TO

Robert Wallace is the pseudonym for Robin
Wallace-Crabbe, who was born in Melbourne
and now lives in the mountains south of
Canberra, New South Wales. A writer and
artist, he has had two novels published in
Australia: *Goanna* and *Feral Palit*, which
received the enthusiastic support of the novelist
Patrick White. *To Catch A Forger* is the first in a
series of thrillers featuring Essington Holt. *An
Axe To Grind* is available as a Gollancz Thriller,
and the third title in the series, *Paint Out*, will be
published by Gollancz in 1990.

TO CATCH A FORGER

by

Robert Wallace

GOLLANCZ CRIME

Gollancz Crime is an imprint of Victor Gollancz Ltd
14 Henrietta Street, London WC2E 8QJ

First published in Great Britain 1988
by Victor Gollancz Ltd

First Gollancz Crime edition 1989

British Library Cataloguing in Publication Data
Wallace, Robert, *1938*–
To catch a forger.
Rn: Robin Wallace-Crabbe   I. Title
823 [F]
ISBN 0-575-04600-7

Printed and bound in Great Britain
by Richard Clay Ltd, Bungay, Suffolk

For Virginia,
who forged a relationship

'The air which one breathes in a picture is not the same as the air one breathes outside.'

Edgar Degas

Chapter 1

There was nothing much in the room: a bed, a stack of dusty paintings against the wall. A blanket was folded on the stained mattress. In the kitchen: a fork, a spoon, a knife, a plate. No saucepans. The potted geraniums had gone from a balcony just wide enough to hold them.

The telephone rang.

'Essington?'

'No.' I replied.

'I've gone, Essington; it had to happen sooner or later.'

'So it's sooner.'

'I knew you'd take it this way. God, you'll never change.'

'We don't, that's what the experts say, we don't.'

'The bond, Essington, we've got to talk about the rent bond.'

'I can't afford to talk about it.'

'I'd thought about that. So you could leave it a month.'

'You're all heart, Annie ... that's what I loved about you: generosity.'

'Someone's got to do something. So it was me.'

'Where do I send it?'

'Well, just for the minute, care of Steffano.'

'Just for the minute?' I hung up.

Steffano. Christ, what a shy lot, running off with each other's best friends. In an adventurous society we'd go for total strangers, but not in swinging Sydney.

Annie was always well-organized, I'll grant her that. It hadn't rubbed off on me, though it had created an illusion of organization in my life. She had got us into the 'studio apartment' in the first place. It would once have been a 'bed-sitter'. She even managed to catch the harbour views between two more piles of dark red brick. She'd climb up on the chair—it was gone too, the chair.

That was my only chair, mahogany, a relic out of Charleston

7

Springs, what mother liked to call 'the family property'. My hand-carved mahogany dining-chair. 'You keep it always, darling; it's a symbol of what we were cheated out of.'

I could visualize Annie. A moment of indecision; then, almost with regret, she'd pick it up, pass it to Steffano and, whoosh, off it went into the van.

They must have used a van. All her books: *Adolescent Aggression*; *Puberty and Public Life*; *Building Blocks of Value*.

What would she tell her charges, her girls? She would be with them now—or would it be afternoon tea-break?—a solid smooth-skinned little form, black hair gleaming, like it was a kind of metal, eyes controlling the unmanageable girls. She was a lion-tamer more than a psychologist.

Now it was Steffano's turn to suffer. He could afford it, suffering. He had the plumbing business and the yacht to keep him out of trouble.

Rent day tomorrow. Good timing, Annie. Rent tomorrow, half the bond in four weeks. That was lots more than I was used to raising at the unavoidable monthly rests.

I rang Steffano.

'Steffano?'

'Steffano, he's not here.'

'Could I leave a message?'

'Yes.' A very demure voice. Wonder what she thought of the boss's new little piece of arse?

'Got a pencil and paper? I want to make sure he gets it.'

'Who shall I say called?'

'Essington Holt.'

'And . . . Mr Holt?'

'You've got the pencil, haven't you?'

'Yes, Mr Holt.'

'Tell him to go fuck himself.'

'I always do, Mr Holt. I assure you, I always do.'

I was stuffed from the trip, stuffed and almost empty-handed. The pictures from the estate of Vincent Jasco seemed like more than the market could handle. Like most things picture market prices are determined by supply and demand. All the Picassos hit the

8

auction room at one time the price collapses; just like potatoes.

Alive, Jasco hardly sold a thing. After death, in 1968, a couple of dealers and the executor of his estate combined efforts to establish a moderate demand. Articles were written; then a small book. Pictures were pushed through the main auctions to advertise increasing prices—round robined. Mainly they were delicate little things, cubist still-life studies, well-mannered, a lot of browns.

A couple of junior Jascos died, then the executor. Suddenly the next generation wanted to clean up. There were the thirty paintings and all they could see was dollars. Thus the auction.

As far as I could make out there were two people bidding, me and a honey-tan smoothie in a hand-stitched linen suit of pale mustard. The auctioneer only had eyes for Mr Suntan. I had to scream out bids to be in the game. After the sixth picture had been knocked down el-quicko to the gavel-banger's blue-eyed boy we took a pause.

'What do you like best?' the competition asked from where he had crept up at my back. He turned me gently with a touch on the shoulder, grinned, held out his hand. 'Jackson.'

'Essington Holt.' We shook.

'It's silly, really, Mr Holt. Pushing each other up. We're just giving away money.'

'That's the system.'

'But it hurts if you don't have the money to give.'

I shrugged. Did I look that bad?

'Which would you like, Mr Holt? Say and it's yours. Just stop bidding.'

'Being honest never got anybody anywhere.' That's what Mother used to say. One of her favourite books was *The Land Boomers*, lists of great Australian families and their managed bankruptcies. 'Your grandfather, he was a proud, honourable man, Essington. But he was a fool. It's the way of the world.'

'The fish on the plate with the key pattern.' A predominantly grey little piece. Poor old Vincent hadn't been too good with colour.

'It's yours, Mr Holt; just give me your card and I'll send it.'

I got his card, writ tiny: Miles Jackson, Consultant, Fine Art.

9

He got my address scrawled on a page torn from the roneoed sale catalogue.

I watched the prices plummet for the next three pictures and left to take the early bus back to Sydney—poor white transport. Maybe I'd just made a couple of thousand dollars, if I could find a buyer. Maybe I'd been conned.

'Father was too cultured for the colonies, that was his problem, too cultured. Rome was his city, he adored Rome. I love it too, they make a wonderful ham sandwich in Rome.' Mother never let up. For her the real culprit was Aunt Eloise.

Aunt Eloise sold up Charleston Springs, gave Mother, her brother's widow, the mahogany dining-table and chairs and hot-footed it to France, cash in hand. There was no real Holt claim to the property . . . it had been built up by the Fabres, who settled in the 1860s. Aunt just happened lucky to marry one: a dwarf who died young. People said all sorts of nasty things about Aunt and her little man but it seems she was very fond of him.

The gesture of giving the table and chairs convinced Mother to claim *de facto* ownership of the entire thing, lock, stock and barrel.

What to eat? The blanket or the pictures? Annie had emptied the fridge, thoughtfully leaving the door open so it didn't get mouldy if I stayed away too long. The electricity was turned off at the main. I cleaned my nails with my pocket knife and thought Essington thoughts.

My poverty was not so real. I had clothes. One pair of sandshoes, one pair of elastic-sided boots, three pale-blue shirts, a tie (black), two tweed sports coats, one pair of flannels, a pair of moleskins, worn jeans, assorted underwear and handkerchiefs.

I took a Norman Lindsay etching to an auction room; a pirate doing something rather nasty to a naked lady. It would be two weeks before the sale and then a few days for the money. I placed a reserve of seven hundred and fifty dollars.

In the bank: four dollars thirty. One thousand, five hundred and sixty-three dollars twenty owing on Bankcard. The rest of my stack of paintings were worth money only if I could convince someone to buy. No real auction-room material: no sheep, no gum trees.

When in trouble touch your friends. Up till now that had meant Steffano—that was before he touched Annie, on the spot it seemed.

Food first . . . that meant Patrick and Peter. Peter was a fugitive from the daily press. At his peak he had been Press Secretary to the Minister for something in somebody's government. The café was his new life. Half his luck, we could all do with one of those—a new life.

Patrick had changed hair from orange to green.

'Duveen, welcome!'

'Maybe not.'

'And why would that be?' asked Peter from the microwave.

'Can I eat on tick?'

'For Christ's sake, what do you think friends are for? Annie pissed off, has she? We sort of knew, didn't we, Pat? What would you like, Ess?'

'Anything that'll go bad if you don't sell it.'

'An omelette then.' Patrick announced. 'Eggs we've got plenty of.'

I sat down pondering the next move—I had to extricate myself from the apartment, bond or no bond. Feathers entered.

It was Feathers who introduced me to Annie: unhappy day. Funny, in the two hours since discovering Annie's departure I had thought, not of her, but of money. Counter to popular theory, no response to being abandoned. It was her skin I liked; her mind was like a steel trap and now its jaws were snapped close about our he-man, Steffano, the plumber.

Mother used to say 'I don't spend all this money on school fees for you to bring home a nobody like that.'

The 'that' was Feathers, a ferrety, wheezing, sand-coloured kid; there only because his father was a clergyman. The Bishop had blessed him with a church in Chippendale. Chippendale—things had changed a bit since then . . . Patrick and Peter had opened Chez Catz, their corner café, neon lights and all. Annie and I had moved into the other side of Broadway, on the border of Ultimo, Pyrmont. Feathers stayed put.

'You are troubled?'

'Never troubled, Feathers. Not Essington.'

11

I was in luck, Feathers was a doer of good works, a barrister–solicitor *extraordinaire*. His office at Richards and Temple was stacked full of the little gems that had passed through my hands. He wrote them off as furniture and, I do believe, he liked them.

'Of course, now I think of it, you're responsible, you're the root of my troubles.'

'Annie?'

'Herself.'

'Only in as much as it was my bathroom you desanctified. I should have had you booked for entering.'

'But you were the host.'

From a ferrety boy Feathers grew into a strapping professional man: polished, discreet, lacking nothing but a fraction of an inch of jaw, more than made up for by his strident Adam's apple.

He was a partner now.

Obsessed by property, Mother had sent me off to work on stations as a jackaroo. While Feathers was passing exams I had been throwing up from the verandahs of bleached hotels; never finding the dreamed-of lost outback heiress—they were saved for the dregs of British aristocracy who added a touch of lisping class at dinner after scrub-up.

If Mother could have seen us now, two men in their mid-forties across a table—a late scene from Hogarth's *Idle and Industrious Apprentice*. Would she have realized that she was wrong? No.

I sometimes wonder if Father ran deliberately into his hail of bullets. Suicide or Mother.

She might not have realized she was wrong but she forgave Feathers for his impoverished background; even developed an obsession with him in her last years, placing her affairs, what there were of them, in his hands. She rang him regularly for advice on the important legal questions of the day, like who was responsible for a rotting paling boundary fence? Or could she force the neighbours to treat their nectarine tree for curly leaf?

So Feathers—Gerald Sparrow—was my family lawyer and, though contemporaries, a kind of father–son relationship developed between us.

'You are a mess, aren't you? How old are you now, Essington?'

'Same as you, Feathers; we were at school together, remember?'

'You may not believe it but I admired you then. You were an inspiration—bursting through the scrum, boxing, no one would get in the ring with you. A killer, remember?'

'What am I supposed to say?'

Patrick brought the omelette. 'On the house for loyal custom past. Mr Sparrow, what would you like?'

'You know what I have, Patrick. I'm not going to change now.'

'Neither am I. So it's toasted ham sandwich and a pot of tea. You are a stick in the mud, aren't you? Look at the blackboard . . . it's a kind of art . . . Peter and I are artists, you know that. And you want toasted ham.'

'Yes, thank you, I do.'

Patrick trotted off, winking at Peter. This was a game played over and over.

'So you're down to botting meals.'

'It's my life.'

I ate in silence. Feathers watched and waited.

'I think I found a nice Vincent Jasco . . . might interest you. A minor masterpiece.'

'What do you mean, "think you've found"?'

So I told him the sordid little story of the auction. He screwed up his nose when I mentioned Miles Jackson, but said nothing.

'Terribly illegal. Haven't you ever bothered to read those conditions of auction? I thought they announced them before selling.'

'But it happens all the time. Common practice.'

'For crooks like Jackson.' Feathers looked disapproving.

'He's just a wheeler-dealer.'

'Don't you believe it.'

'Does that mean I don't get my picture?'

'Oh no, it should turn up. Why not? He got the other twenty-nine.'

'And would you be interested?'

'I'll take a look. What's it worth?'

'Fifteen hundred, two thousand . . . two thousand to you.' I joked.

'And you could do with the money.'

'I could do with the money, correct.'

Feathers wrote out a cheque and gave me fifty dollars cash.

'Here's an advance on the Jasco. No picture and you pay it back, clear?'

He really did like my mother. Misread her completely. Funny that. The way people take to other people's mothers.

I wonder if Annie had a mother?

Chapter 2

The phone rang.

'Mr Holt?' It was Steffano's telephone lady.

'Yes.'

'Hold the line a minute please.'

'Essington?' It was the ladies'-man plumber.

'Steffano, nice of you to call.'

'Look, Essington. OK, you feel hard done by. Maybe we should have come straight out, been more open with you. But I can't have you talking filth to my staff. They're separate—it's like another life, OK.' Annie had already destroyed what mind Steffano Polini had. Poor sucker.

'Essington, the kid I've got here on the telephone, she's a really nice girl, pretty too. Well, she was shocked to have to pass your filth on to me. She said you insisted that she write it down.'

'That was so she wouldn't have to mouth the words. Take it from me, Steffano, I don't like to defile the innocent.'

'OK. Well, Annie and I have talked this out. We decided that you give us a bit of air for a couple of months. You understand, Essington—for Annie's sake. She can't take too much pressure. You know that, for Christ's sake!'

'You say this girl's a really nice girl? I'm sorry to talk bad to her, Steffano. I thought she was your mother.'

'Arsehole.'

I planted the phone. Steffano was all gleaming Mediterranean muscle but piss weak. He could be fun. We had a lot of good nights together. But he'd been into the phone box for a change and the real Steffano had come out. No superman.

I rang his number, got the girl with the voice.

'Essington Holt.'

'You want Mr Polini?'

15

'No. Look, I'm really sorry to have used a word like "fuck" to a nice girl like you. I even made you write it down.'

'That's all right, Mr Holt, I just shut my eyes and all the nasty things go away.'

'I wanted to apologize. To make amends. I was confused, didn't know what I was saying.'

'That's very nice of you, Mr Holt.'

'What are you doing tonight?'

'First, Mr Holt, I'm going to a prayer meeting, then I wrap food parcels for the poor till I drop off to sleep.'

'How about leg wrestling instead?'

'Sounds good. What time?'

Karen lived on the North Shore. She had a beautiful view of the Pacific Highway. The noise level was so high we wouldn't have slept even if we'd wanted to.

Tired but happy we rose for breakfast.

We threw down a couple of cups of instant coffee. She lit a good-day sunshine cigarette; idiot happy voices prattled away on the radio occasionally interrupted by disco-beat pop.

We squeezed into a train. I pecked her on the cheek and got out at Martin Place.

'I'll ring.'

'Do.'

'So long, Karen. Give the boss hell.'

'I will.'

People and doors curtained us from each other. I felt as though I had stepped outside and left her a part of a solid lump that was Sydney.

I deposited the cheque at nine-thirty, walked to Hunter Street and was waiting at the second-floor glass door of Miles Jackson's establishment right on ten o'clock.

A fat-cheeked little man opened up at ten-ten. I followed him inside and started examining the collection hanging on rough silk walls.

The little man fussed about at his desk. Opened drawers, shut them, answered the phone a couple of times and then, composed by ritual, approached.

'Can I help you?'

'Well, I hope so. The name's Holt. I'd like to see Mr Jackson.'

'It's a little early for Mr Jackson. He works mornings from his residence.'

'Maybe you could help. It's about a Jasco he bought on my behalf in Melbourne a couple of days ago.'

I didn't expect it to be there. I guess I was just checking after Feathers' disapproval. Mindlessly checking.

'We expect them today, by air. I could ring him if you like.'

'If you would.'

I wasn't really looking the part. A waxed girl, Karen did not own a razor. My flannels had crumpled under the weight of a spilled doona—the ubiquitous fad quilt that was making sleepers sweat through hot Sydney nights.

I felt worse than I looked, set against that little image of perfection, brass reefer-jacket buttons shining.

'Miles, I've a Mr . . . What did you say your name was again?'

'Holt.'

'A Mr Holt.'

I smiled down the magic lines to Mr Jackson. Fat cheeks stared straight through me.

'Yes Miles, just wait, I'll write that down . . . no . . .' He made notes. They had clearly passed from me to more important matters.

I examined the collection—pricey stuff, mostly out of my league. A couple of Glovers, one dubious; a lovely small Boucher drawing; two Bunny oils, one unfinished; a Degas monotype; several nineteenth-century bronzes of the kind that provided acceptable soft porn; and a large, boring, late Streeton landscape. Scattered in among that lot were more modest works to which I could learn to aspire, including an Ellis Rowan flowerpiece that I had bought and sold several years back.

Fat cheeks hung up.

'Will you be at home this afternoon?'

'Just.'

He let that pass. 'It will be delivered at four sharp.'

'Thank you. I will be expecting it. How much for the pseudo Degas?'

17

'Hardly pseudo, Mr Holt. And I suspect a little out of range, yours and mine.'

They could keep the bed and shove the phone—it was in Annie's name, she had insisted. Paintings and all else were in my two-wheeler suitcase by the door. Bonds, rent in lieu of notice, the whole thing was beyond my powers of concentration.

'How old are you, Essington?' I could hear myself asking. It was twenty to four.

I rang Feathers at his office. He was out. I wanted to ring long distance or, better still, international. There was only Aunt at Cap Ferrat; I hardly knew Aunt. No, there was no way I could monster the account. I didn't care. I didn't really hate them; Steffano and Annie, brave together on life's rocky road.

Smack on four the painting came. 'Courtesy Miles Jackson, Consultant, Fine Art.'

'One day,' I promised myself, 'I'm not going to get a card like that.'

I took a room at the Whitfield, a genteel rooming-house for the *déclassé* poor, looking down on the harbour at Double Bay— Annie's water view at last. I left the reception-desk number with Feathers' secretary and retired to the TV room to watch *The Road Runner*.

He's reliable, Feathers; it goes with his appearance. He rang at a quarter to seven.

'It's a sweat shop, haven't you got a union?' I asked.

'We are a union, haven't you heard? Glad you called, I tried to reach you earlier. I've a letter, it came to the office.'

'For me?'

'For you, wherever you're hiding.'

'Must be for Mother.'

'Your mother's dead, Essington. She will not return.'

'Who would write to you for me?'

'The person who wrote the letter.'

I never knew Feathers had a car. Never saw him in one before. And what a car, a Porsche 356 shining like new despite its thirty-odd years. Full marks to the painter, Derain, who at the height of his

18

fame said, 'I never saw a painting as beautiful as a motor car'. Only Derain said that in French. Maybe it sounds better that way. I'd forgotten lots of school French. I remembered '*Je vous aime beaucoup*'. It's out of a song. I didn't really recall what a *beaucoup* was.

Porsche never made a car after the 356—not one so dashing, so romantic.

'Suits you, the Whitfield,' Feathers said. 'I would seriously counsel making a long-term booking.'

'I was thinking just the same myself. And in the afternoons, guess what? Cartoons on the telly.'

Feathers almost cracked a smile.

I had been waiting in the street. He would have got lost in the corridors. The Whitfield, for all its charm, is not the sort of place where you can expect a bell-boy as a guide.

For driving, pigskin gloves with perforated backs were accessories to the legal suit.

'Would you like to come in and look at the painting?'

'Why don't you bring it out, Essington, and I'll spirit you away from this your final resting place for a couple of hours.'

'The letter?'

He passed me the envelope.

'France,' he said. 'I could tell by the stamps.'

'You can't fool me, you steamed it open.'

'Cross my heart and hope to die.'

The restaurant was selected for the drive, I thought. Feathers executed natty little gear shifts and angled corners as though competing in the Adelaide Grand Prix. Speedwise we sat on a steady thirty miles per hour. No screaming tyres.

'Isn't she a beauty? Your mother would have approved of this, Essington.'

Feathers never said 'Essington' straight. Or rather, he said it too straight. Still, I let him have his little pleasures. A more admirable man I had never met even if he wasn't a heap of fun. Where either the opposite or the same sex was concerned I think he must have been saving himself up for the geriatric hospital; I gather there's tons of slap and tickle there.

We finished up at The Pelican, facing the sea at Brighton-le-

Sands—or that's what the neon spelt out above the big-beaked bird.

'Evening, Mr Sparrow,' and a nod of the head at me: 'Sir'—disapproving. As though I was a rapist that Mr Sparrow was obliged to save from just deserts.

'Your usual table by the window.'

'Splendid, splendid.' Feathers was rubbing his hands. Where had he learnt to live these lives? That mousey little boy, that brunt of boys' grammar-school cruelty?

'Well, Essington, read your letter. We're all agog to know what's what. You have an aunt in France, remember. Your mother, God rest her soul, might have mentioned her.'

He loved playing his father role with me.

'Some lovely crays tonight, Mr Sparrow. And the gars couldn't be fresher.'

We got a menu each along with the specialist advice.

'You wouldn't believe it would you. It's Aunt.'

'Eloise isn't it? She stole the family fortune.'

'That's what Mother said.'

'Would you like a little something to start? What we call in polite circles, an aperitif.'

'A whisky.'

'Why don't you try a Kir or better still we'll have a Kir Royale. Er, Mrs Patterson, two Kir Royale—Moët et Chandon—have one yourself and leave the bottle.' He leant forward. 'This, Essington, but you mustn't tell anyone, is the best restaurant in Sydney. They do things better down here. More money you see; the mortgages are smaller.

'And we must do the best we can because I believe this is your farewell dinner.'

Chapter 3

'Dear Karen, love you and leave you, regards to God, hell to Steffano Polini. I am doomed for France. Love Essington.'

One up on the Melbourne–Sydney bus. It was my first time out of Australia to 'overseas'. UTA, you pay a little extra if you want champagne. Extraordinary feeling heading off to the world's other side where history is made and broken. Out the window, scrub turning to desert and all those pubs and stockyards and miles and miles of dust: Mother's pastoral paradise.

I just loved it. Loved the force feeding, the 'F' grade movies, the stops and starts. For the first time ever my life was lifted clean out of my hands. As far as I was concerned we were either up there or boom. There was nothing to fix. A plane isn't a world held together with improvisation. It's like God: all there or not at all. So total that it doesn't matter either way.

Feathers had let me read the letter out to him while he nodded approval. But he knew the story already. Aunt Eloise had contacted his firm to trace me . . . she had, in her time, received dotty correspondence through them from Mother as she spiralled downhill, a cheated woman.

Aunt Eloise Fabre had sold up quickly after the death of her little love. It had been towards the end of the Korean War. Wool and therefore land prices were high. She took the money with her to France, bought a villa overlooking the Mediterranean and put the rest of the loot across a range of investments. She indulged a love of art and got together a collection of small masterpieces— this had always been part of the myth of Aunt Eloise: the Sisley, the Picasso, the two small Matisse nudes, the Rodin bronze, and the six rare Degas.

'Bought with our money, that's how she got them. By rights the whole lot is ours,' Mother would say.

Oops, there went Australia's north-western edge. It had

given way to the sea you go over to be overseas.

It was the talk of Aunt and art that got me going. The bush was a dead loss, a wasteland of dirt and mutton fat and mindless bravado. Even I wanted to take a peep over the edge after a while. What interested me was pictures—fascinated my mind. Why were the good ones so good, the bad ones terrible? Why were there a few that you could look at forever? So I bought some, sold some, mainly concentrating on translocation: what goes in Sydney doesn't in Melbourne and vice versa. In theory there isn't an easier way to make money. The only hitch is you have to find the buyers and in general buyers like to deal with the Miles Jacksons of our world, Cartier lighters and all.

I knew people looked at pictures, everybody knew that. It was Aunt putting a couple of thousand of her acres into art that was a model of the stuff's commercial potential. The rest, everything beyond the idea, I guess I got wrong.

For reasons of her own, at seventy, widowed twice (the second a retired British officer attracted, Mother said, by our money), Aunt had got a fraction paranoic.

'That's your letter, Essington. I didn't want to spoil your fun. My letter fills in the gaps.'

'Oh! there's a "your letter" too, is there?'

'Of course. Mrs Patterson!' She approached through the maze of vacant chairs and tables. 'Her husband, Hubert, does the cooking, it's a kind of hobby with him. Oh, Mrs Patterson, I was just telling my friend here what a splendid cook your husband is.'

'Yes, well he loves it, doesn't he, Mr Sparrow?'

'Empty house tonight, Mrs Patterson.'

'Usual for a Tuesday, Mr Sparrow. I said: "Why don't we shut Tuesdays?" And Hubert, he said: "What would we do then, Rabbit?" That's like a pet name for me you see. "What would we do Tuesdays, Rabbit? You've got your booze, I've got me pots and pans." And you know, Mr Sparrow, Hubert's right.'

'We were put here to suffer and to labour, Mrs Patterson. What would you suggest to go with the gar?'

'We've still got a bit of the Chablis you like so much. Very dear but it really is nice. And we got a couple of boxes of a lovely Hermitage Blanc . . . you might like to try that for a change.'

'One of each thank you, Mrs Patterson. But you've got to help us out and take a glass or two . . . Essington, as you may or may not recall, my father ended his days in a little retirement development for the Church's loyal servants in Tasmania, just outside Launceston—Glover country, your territory now.'

'Wish it was.'

'Thank you, Mrs Patterson. No, just pour; you are my guide, Mrs Patterson.' She pulled the cork, poured a drop into a glass from the next table, rolled the pale gold fluid about in her mouth.

'I visited him there, close to the end of his days, and a curious thing occurred. Every night of the month I spent there I dreamed of childhood. He was inhabiting his childhood, I mine. He because of age; in my case, it was either out of sympathy or the result of geographical dislocation. I believe it was the latter. The illusion of adult games, they seem so real. Don't they mask the fact that we are children always?

'Ah lovely, Mrs Patterson. A true masterpiece and in equal company: Mr Patterson's gars.'

'Where does Aunt come in, Feathers?'

'The tone of her letters. There have been three though she never answered those posted on your poor mother's behalf—evidence of judgement, perhaps! She is beginning to mistrust any sense of belonging in her rich but foreign world. Step one, seek the advice and assistance of compatriots.'

'Why? Feathers, what expert advice could I offer? Her kind of art is outside my experience. It's the art of books.'

'That may be true, Essington. Yet people with just as much familiarity with European masters run our major galleries, they are quoted in the papers. An expert, or rather to be expert, Essington, is an inner state.'

'So I look at her art . . .'

'And see if it's the proper stuff. You see your aunt suspects that there has been a switch, some of the paintings might not be the originals she bought all those years ago.'

'You need X-rays, all kinds of laboratory gear.'

'Or, Essington, a pure heart.'

'Underqualified on all counts.'

'But more than anything she seems to need to see someone; to have a family connection.'

'Thus the tickets, thus the retainer?'

'Exactly. Actually I think she intended Business Class for flesh and blood. I thought you might use the difference on clothes and sit with the jet-set *hoi polloi*.'

Feathers insisted on joining in the shopping spree. They were all his acquaintances, the prissy little men who managed to stuff my heavy shoulders into powder-blue linen, a stern dark suit of Italian cloth, soft-collared shirts. 'Oh Lord,' I thought, 'I am not worthy.' A little extra cash adjusted trouser lengths and let out seams. I'm a solid boy and despite all their care it seemed to me in the mirrors that the sad cow-brown-eyed head was not transformed set on top of tailor's artworks.

Reading a French phrase book is a sure way to avoid conversation on a UTA flight, unless someone wants to practise English. I just sat there, a bulky, natty man, and consumed. I had been saved by the bell—a stroke of luck; it would only happen once.

The Vincent Jasco I got from Miles Jackson paid out Bankcard—Feathers had loved the picture. The card itself was cut in two by a bank teller with a pair of scissors before my very eyes and replaced with a smarter, more international gold number in keeping with my new status.

By take-off time I felt that any more of Feathers' nursing would cause suffocation—Porsche 356 and all.

Paris had its fifth bomb attack in eleven days, just twelve hours before touchdown at Charles de Gaulle. I passed through their anti-terrorist net without problem, was bussed to the city's southern side, then cooled my heels at Orly waiting for the plane to Nice. So much for the world's cultural capital—a glimpse of mansard roofs basking in white sunshine and millions of small dented cars whizzing about on the wrong side of the road.

I did discover I had told myself a lie. I had more French than I realized. It started returning from school-days. French and Art had been my only subjects and all because of hated Aunt Eloise. Not much French, mind you, but the odd word, written, made sense.

*

'Aunt, you sure it's not Cary Grant next door?'

A slim, slightly aged figure in impeccable white strolling among gum trees.

Mother would have stepped over the red line if she had actually seen how Aunt Eloise lived. Judgement: she had known when to get out and where to go.

Rebecca laid out the table for breakfast, so well-trained there was no need—it might have been an insult—to notice her constant, silent domestic service. I had a rather Napoleon III room with a terrace all to itself.

Tea, bacon and eggs, toast and marmalade.

'Do you have the sliced bread flown in?'

'Don't you be naughty, Essington. Very modern people, the French.'

Rebecca must have dined out on stories of exotic Australian cuisine. If she ever escaped, that was. A ride-on mower was being jockeyed between us and Mr Cary Grant look-alike. Through the trees, the lighthouse, the turquoise sea forever, then Libya.

My third breakfast in paradise during which I earned my keep reading out the most significant events reported in the *Herald Tribune*.

Renardo had taken me *très vite* to Italy, about half an hour away, in the Bentley Continental, a relic of time past, and irreplaceable. He was showing me the world. I sat, very Roger Moore, in my blue linen and a natty little pair of rope-sole shoes I picked up along the way, wondering how my ankles would go without support from traditional Australian elastic-sides.

Renardo, like Rebecca, seemed to make a point of being a non-person. Aunt Eloise's was a separate existence. Feathers may not have been far from the mark with his amateur analysis.

'The mere fact, Essington, of living in another country indicates nothing. My mind belongs back there at Charleston. You see, that was my home. But it was too painful to stay there and my first husband . . . he was a clever man, Essington, he insisted that I promise to sell it the moment he died. "If you're not master of it," he said, "a property like this can drag you down." He assured me it would never be that price again. Of course he was right.'

More tea and toast. I was going to end up tubby Essington under such a regime. Dinner had been roast New Zealand lamb, roast vegetables, mint sauce. Only the wine was French. Mrs Patterson would have loved the wine.

'Nephew, I don't want you to rush about making a fuss. Just relax and enjoy yourself.'

That afternoon I walked off the promontory that was Cap Ferrat and followed the beach around for a swim at Villefranche. A couple of US warships swung at anchor in the bay. The water was clean, salty and supportive. I swam the bay for exercise then laid my body down to rest in the sun.

Walking home I crossed over to the Beaulieu side of Cap Ferrat, noted the existence at Beaulieu's Baie des Fourmis of an imaginative late nineteenth-century rotunda advertising regular art auctions, and then walked via St Jean-Cap-Ferrat back to Aunt's villa. In this resting place of the rich nobody walks, nobody but sightseers that is.

Cary look-alike did nothing but stare out to sea in his whites. Renardo trundled about on the mower when not chauffeuring at the Continental's wheel or occupied on more mundane automotive exercises in Aunt's diesel Citroën brake.

For the first time in my life I was feeling overpaid and underworked. Usually, since the bush, I was just underworked.

Sipping pre-dinner champagne: 'Talk to me about the pictures.'

'Aunt Eloise, I don't like to say this, but I've a nasty feeling that you know a hell of a lot more about the pictures than I do.'

'But it's your life, Essington.'

'It was supposed to be. Didn't turn out much, though.'

We were walking the first-floor gallery. On one side a phoney Renaissance balustrade of pink marble giving on to the black and white tiled central lobby; on the other, walls through which doors opened into sitting-rooms and bedrooms. Between these doors hung the pictures, far more of them than had existed in the Australian story.

'At the time they really were so very cheap. I just couldn't help myself. You know, Essington, you can feel in your bones if a thing's too cheap. You've just got to know a few basic commodity prices for comparison. This Braque etching, if I remember rightly, cost quite a bit less than a television set when I bought it. Actually, it's quite rare. Not one of those things turned out in the ateliers and then signed.'

I peered at the crude nude form on a scratched and pitted copper plate that had been transferred to paper. Pretty exciting even for a feller like me, past his prime. This was the real stuff.

There was an elegant Léger gouache, quite late; the Sisley—poplars by water, delicate and fresh, two people drifting on the water in a boat.

'You like that?'

'Yes I do. From reproductions I've always preferred him to Monet.'

'You are a funny boy, Essington. I'm damned if I can find anything of my brother in you. He was spiky, aggressive always, no time to think.'

'I've got the time, all the time in the world. I've never been particularly good at it.'

'Let's see what you think of these then.'

She opened the door into a dressing-room. Small really. The furniture, Empire.

They were a cluster above a black and gold lacquer chest, six of them, two rows of three. Lovely little Degas monotypes, brothel scenes, masterly drawing, heads in almost Egyptian profile. Small black and white images very simply framed in a fine black moulding, maybe thirty millimetres wide.

A guzzler, Aunt walked back along the gallery to where Rebecca had left the bottle in its silver bucket.

Pinch me, was I dreaming?

Since escaping the bush I had tried twice to learn to paint. First time I struck a bunch of mindless lefties who had taken over an art school. They had wanted nothing more or less than Khomeniesque obedience from rooms of their devotees. They were paid salaries that could have fed small third-world countries. I lasted a term and it took everything I've got to keep my hands off one particularly nasty piece of work who mixed sarcasm with a rehash of the thoughts of Chairman Mao. I wanted to draw; that was what I thought I could do.

Next I tried private classes but ran out of money before my talent reared its ugly head. Other than that, over the years, I've done a bit of reading, looking, and have found it necessary to learn about methods and materials used. Up the bush I did a lot of sketching around the stations.

I had read accounts of Degas's pastel technique and of his monotypes. He managed results in both media that have eluded artists before and since.

Not girlie pictures, the brothel scenes, but not moralizing either. Slightly comic, I suppose. Well-observed images of the people of the *belle époque*. Observations of brothel manners—Feathers might have thought that a 'contradiction in terms'. He liked to use that phrase, Feathers. In thinking he had been my mentor as in most things else. Better late than never, let that be my motto.

'Well, Essington?'

'Look good to me, Aunt. But you must remember that I know more about horses than I do about Degas.'

'There was a studio sale after his death. But these were not from there.'

'Yes, I read about that.'

What I didn't like to say just then was that I had seen one of the six pictures before, hanging on the wall of the Sydney fine art consultant, Miles Jackson.

Chapter 4

'Do you mind if I take one down? I'd like to look at the back.'

I took down the Miles Jackson model. It had been set in the frame not so long ago.

'They've all recently been done.'

'Oh!' I said. Aunt was watching for reactions while holding the Rothschild *grand cru* by the neck.

'Yes, that's part of the reason why you're here. I'd swear they aren't the same pictures, not the ones I bought.'

Degas was famed for his antisocial behaviour. He could act the comic, there are photos of him playing up, but generally he was a grumpy old recluse. Rich, a collector, close.

Knowledge of his works is based on uncertain documentation. His little monotypes are considered a particular aspect of his work; the most intimate, the most revealing of his thought process. The brothel monotypes were very private works that only came to light after his death. Picasso had a set. But what is a set?

Degas's monotypes were produced by drawing direct in ink and rubbing back on highly polished copper plates. The finished image was then printed under pressure through a press.

You only get one print—thus 'monotype'. In most cases you wonder why an artist would bother. Degas, a master of drawing, chose the medium for its ability to permit him to rub out, add, rub out again—working with maximum fluidity until he could print and thus fix what he had.

There was no way for the same image to be in Sydney and in Aunt's villa at Cap Ferrat all at the same time.

Dinner was a salmon kedgeree of a kind still served, perhaps, in outlying bush hospitals; washed down with a bottle and a half of 1971 Châteauneuf-du-Pape. For Aunt a meal was an excuse for boozing.

'They're fakes, that's what they are, all fakes. I've been had, Essington.'

'But how? You've had them for years.'

'I've been had. Old age. An old woman alone. The bastards went for me.'

She splashed the table with the refill.

'Insurance, Essington, is an unnecessary evil. We believe in them. We send them photographs; it's considered silly not to. All so we get the money if something gets nicked.'

She was slurring.

'Who's to know if it's not those insurance Johnnies who nick them? Oh, the nicest, absolutely the most plausible man, butter wouldn't melt in his mouth. A true French gentleman. Don't you believe all that English talk; the French can be charming. This is civilization, here, the Riviera . . . Civilization, Essington.'

We knocked back a couple of Cognacs per head with coffee for me, jasmine tea for Aunt Eloise.

'Just talking about it makes me feel better, angrier but better. You're worth the fare for that alone.'

'Thank you, Aunt. But are you sure? They look good to me. It's not easy, something like a monotype. The line would have to be so certain.'

'They are not the same pictures. I know my Degas; they've been my companions for over thirty years, those saucy girls, those debauchees; they were my little characters. I knew their winks, their grins, their frowns.'

Compensation for living in an exotic paradise: I wasn't stuck with a wowser; Aunt wasn't morally disapproving.

After next morning's Australian breakfast and readings from the *Herald Tribune*, concluded with a ritual chant of fine print—currency values, commodity prices and share indices— I extracted more detail from my employer–aunt.

All insurance was taken out through a Monaco broker and the policies were Lloyds. Paintings and individual items of furniture had been documented and valued as acquired with coverage added to the policy. All that without change for thirty years, handled by a

Mr Swann-Baker, friend it seems of the late Colonel, Aunt's number two.

They must have thought they were on to something, the Colonel and his crony: two upper-crust English spivs. 'That,' Feathers would have said, 'is a tautology.'

Everything went fine. Four years ago God took the Colonel and two years later poor old Swann-Baker rushed off upstairs to join his cobber at the great tailor shop in the sky.

New broom sweeps clean. Bright eyed and bushy tailed, it seems, Georges Pagés stepped into the breach. One of the new people.

Pagés wanted photos for the file and redocumentation to feed into a computer on the machine's own terms.

Aunt didn't like it. Once you have a painting, she believed, best leave it rest where you put it. There was a fight during which she sent a first letter to Richards and Temple where it trickled down to the youngest partner, Gerald Sparrow, my feathered friend. Why Richards and Temple? Because of Mother's letters. They gave her the name, there was a family connection, 'tenuous perhaps, Essington, but it existed.'

After a lot of toing and froing, Aunt, on Feathers' advice, ditched the London lawyers who seemed to be taking the part of the insurance company. This was a firm connected by blood to the late Colonel and to his first cousin the Earl of—, who must remain nameless because earls are a known quantity.

An Australian corporation lawyer connected to a Monaco bank took on Aunt, freelance, as a favour to Richards and Temple who retained a portion of him for work involving French connections.

He got on to Pagés and a compromise was struck. Redocumentation and photographs, yes. But at home, in Villa du Phare.

All's well that ends well and this ended badly. The experts took two days to complete what Aunt had thought would be a twenty-minute job. She was obliged to leave them alone a lot of the time, even though they were 'flashy and rude'.

She rang Pagés hourly, complaining, as his two henchmen worked their way through the house. Col Winter—Richards and Temple's, and therefore, Feathers' man—was in Geneva for the week, conveniently uncontactable. His office was sympathetic but unhelpful.

Renardo and Rebecca had been seconded to keep tabs on the operators but it was long, laborious and confusing with lights, a secretary typing as they worked and cameras blazing away. At the end of the second day they left. They had clocked up a lot of expensive hours.

Eight days later, unexpectedly, someone returned. Aunt was out being driven in the Bentley up into the mountains for a day's change of air. It was one of the gentlemen who had been there the week before. Rebecca let him in, assuming the visit to be part of the work. She was told that one film had failed to come out—a fault of the camera. He stayed for a couple of hours retaking shots that should have been recorded on the botched film. She had left him to it.

When she returned, Aunt was horrified to learn of the revisit. She rushed up to the dressing-room. Her Degas were not the same pictures. She could see that. But only she—to Rebecca and Renardo they were exactly the same. But, 'What did servants know or care?'

There was nobody else familiar with the works. Scholars had not seen them, maybe ever. Only Swann-Baker's old fuddy-duddy cronies had and they were long dead.

'Feathers,' I screamed through time and space, 'how do you prove that a thing's a fake?'

And the answer came out of the air, not so much from Feathers as from God, as Cary Grant took his first garden stroll of the day.

'My son, you find the fucking forger, don't you?'

Georges Pagés was very much your friend and mine, greeting me in his one-desk, no-frills office on the Boulevard de Suisse. All trace of Swann-Baker was erased.

Renardo had a couple of errands on the Menton side of Monte Carlo and would pick me up at a coffee bar on the Quai des États-Unis in two hours.

Pagés liked the way he spoke English. He was a kind of do-it-yourself Rossano Brazzi kit. Warmth, he had learnt warmth; maybe did postgraduate work in it.

'The saga of Mrs Fabre.' Aunt had always kept her first husband's name.

'That's the one.'

'But it's over now, everything is right. They are in a computer. Now, you see, instead of worrying Mrs Fabre, all we need to do is adjust value against market indications. Dr Winter, here in Monaco, he is satisfied, though a most fastidious man. I am happy, my masters are happy.'

'And what about the client?'

'Mrs Fabre is an old woman. We must expect these things. Business, Mr 'olt, is not just business. There is psychology also. We must understand each other if we are to deal with each other.'

'Is that a quote?'

'I beg your pardon.'

'I thought, maybe de Gaulle?' I smiled to let him off the hook but it was clear that his psychology did not extend to digs at national heroes.

'I tried to contact Mr Winter.'

'Dr Winter.'

'Sorry, doctor. He wasn't in so I came to you, Mr Pagés.' You could see him wince at the way I said his name. 'Mrs Fabre is my aunt, I'm her loving nephew all the way from Australia in the *Pacifique Sud*. I just want to put her mind at ease.'

'But, there is nothing more that I can do, I run a business. I can't stop everything for Mrs Fabre.'

'I don't want you to. Still, she's going to feel a lot better just because we've talked. Psychology, Mr Pagés.'

'Pagés.' He corrected my pronunciation, making full use of the accent.

'Sorry, Pagés. What would put her at her ease would be for me to chat to the chaps who did the work.'

'The work?'

'Who made the photographs, did the documentation.'

'But, surely, Mr 'olt, these people are very reliable.'

'It's only to get an old lady off your back. Actually, Pagés, it's Holt, there's an 'h'.'

The experts were at Nice. Working out of Galerie de la Renaissance, Rue de France, one back from the seafront and the Promenade des Anglais. It was one of many with pretty pictures in

33

even prettier frames sitting in the window; a sort of rogues' alley, but genteel rogues.

I had a little trouble explaining to Renardo that this was our next stop. We were not announcing our arrival with the Bentley Continental. He parked the Citroën brake right outside to sit while I took care of business.

Mr Galerie de la Renaissance looked like a left-over Riviera movie extra—silk shirt unbuttoned just so to display brown chest with gold cross as decoration. His hair was bleached yellow; the only tell-tale signs of age were around the eyes and the shaggy eyebrows.

In amongst the junk, ancient and modern, hung a genuine looking Marquet, a painting of Deauville or some place like that: greys and blobs of mixed-down colour.

My friend batted eyelids: that was the long and the short of hello.

I hovered over the Marquet for a respectable period of time, walked out to the car, convinced a stubborn Renardo to drive off and take a coffee somewhere. He was to pick me up along the gallery stretch around six. I wanted Mr Renaissance to think that I was somebody—driver and all. Important, these things.

I looked some more at the Marquet while my friend shifted position into line of sight should I lift my eyes.

I did; he caught me. Wasn't that nice?

'Good little Marquet.'

'You like it?' What a charming smile. It must have been the cross, the neck line, the gold wrist bangle, Aunt thought vulgar . . . maybe not the cross.

'Well, I do, yes. Very nice indeed.'

We eyed each other. He didn't think I wanted his Marquet. I didn't think so either. So I went straight in and talked about my aunt.

He was sweet. No hesitation. The story was just like hers only none of the pictures were lifted. 'Of course, such a charming lady. We could see we were upsetting her but what could we do? The valuations, they're part of our business. It's always a curious situation one way or another, an embarrassment.'

'I can imagine.' I liked this sham. He was describing things the way they are.

34

'You're where you're not wanted or you value too low or you're too high, pushing up the premium. You can't win. So you develop a hide like a . . .'

'Like a rhinoceros.'

'Exactly Mr . . .?'

'Holt.'

' 'olt. My name is Thompson . . . Jean-Pierre Thompson.'

'Essington. Pleased to meet you.'

The photographers worked out of Cannes. They were sorry about the return visit. Nothing like that had happened before. It was the shutter, something wrong with the shutter; there was a vertical white smudge up one side of all the shots on the last cassette.

Would I like to see them? He still had them to keep as a record. 'I keep everything, it's something psychological. I guess that's why I'm a collector.'

'I thought you sold.'

'A collector, a dealer. The same mentality.'

We were chatting amicably on the street when Renardo came cruising.

Thompson was happy to be of service. 'Old ladies are not old ladies, Mr 'olt, they are people. I would have worried too if our positions were reversed.'

Even speaking English with a strong American accent he couldn't get an 'h' into Holt. And what could I do with Thompson to repay the compliment?

'You've been a great help and thank you. There's only one thing.'

'The Marquet, I hope.'

'Sorry, no. Just before I left Australia I saw something close to a perfect copy of one of those Degas. Hanging on a dealer's wall. How could that be?'

'It was his way of working. Degas, he repeated the same image again and again.'

'Is that it? We don't know much about these things out there in the *Pacifique Sud*.' But, I thought, we know that's not true . . . some of us at any rate.

Six cars had got stuck behind Renardo and a delivery truck also

35

double parked on the other side of the one-way street. There was a whole lot of tooting going on.

We shook hands and I leapt into my red chariot to be spirited away on soft hydraulics through the old port, around Mount Boron, along the arc of the beach of Villefranche to the Boulevard Général de Gaulle, home and the lighthouse.

Cary was standing on his balcony in the warm glow of a late summer afternoon, his togs reflecting light. Was he real or did they wind him up to run on rails?

Chapter 5

Tipsy from dinner, I sat out on my balcony for a bit of the what's-it-all-about-Essington.

Those Europeans had a thing or two to teach a boy from New South Wales. On reflection it seemed to me that they had been understanding and even a little charming. Twice in a day I had confronted total strangers, more or less inferring that they were part of a plot to swindle my old aunt. They hadn't thrown me out the door as they may well have been entitled to do. Mr Pagés had explained as pleasantly as time allowed that there was a psychological side to life. The very international Mr Thompson had held back on nothing.

The puzzle, was it in Aunt Eloise's mind? Not in the pictures?

I had rushed in, excited by adventure, into a world of which I knew nothing. I couldn't tell a fake Degas if I fell over one. Neither perhaps could Aunt. She couldn't even read the paper. She had bought me instead of glasses. That blind, how could she pick out the detail she loved in her tiny monotypes? Answer, she couldn't. There was no mystery, no swindle. Just a bunch of professionals dealing as best they could with a difficult, lonely old woman.

My problem was to convince her that the pictures were the ones she bought all those years ago. My job was that of a psychologist not of an art expert. I was ill-suited to both.

With considerable disappointment I could see an early end to my little luxurious adventure. Midnight would strike and I would turn back into a Sydney pumpkin or frog or something—maybe not a frog.

After breakfast I walked from the lighthouse to the Plage de Passable for my daily swim, a kilometre or so over to Villefranche. I aimed for the old port. It was from here, years ago, that the ships of the kings of Sardinia had set out to war. Half-way across I turned around a mooring buoy and headed for the beach. You can't do this in Sydney Harbour if you don't want to feed the sharks.

At two o'clock I was dropped at Beaulieu by Renardo who was taking Aunt to Monaco to fiddle about with her fortune, or to see a doctor, or Dr Winter. Maybe he was into psychology too? It's got to a stage where the only person who isn't a doctor is your doctor who's a naturopath or herbalist or reads your eyes. Things changing and Essington falling behind.

There was an auction at the rotunda and I was hoping to pick up a Picasso for a dollar.

It's important to overcome disappointment at what's put up for sale at auctions. Art's a pyramid with a huge base. There were a lot of paintings of naked ladies looking silly with nothing to do but be naked, and cases of valuable bric-à-brac, snuffboxes, pomade jars, dubious classical fragments and the heads or hands of saints nicked from churches behind the clergy's backs—or by the clergy.

There were drawings ambiguously presented with attributions but no provenance. There are a number of people in Australia who supplement their income producing that sort of thing, a casual drawing that could be a John Singer Sargent—you need skill to do it.

At the upper level a forger can make a lot of money. About fifteen years ago a major private American collection was sent to Canada on loan. While there almost every piece was declared a fake. On recrossing the border the works were no longer designated works of art and duty was charged. That's the sort of experience I have, stories that you get from books on the forger's art. But I couldn't pick a fake, not if it was good.

Beaulieu is a watering place reserved, by popular consent, for the successful old of England. The hotel dominating the bay is called The Bedford. There are palm trees, parks, an antique shop selling postcards and maps on the side. You'd be pretty safe with who you met at The Bedford.

Mixed in with the stooped winners of life were the art spivs—me, I guess, included—there only for the day of the sale. In the back of my mind was the hope of bumping into Jean-Pierre; it had occurred to me to apologize for impudence. There were look-alikes but no real McCoy.

Once bidding started I was lost. I couldn't follow the numbers—could have been tens or thousands. Still, it was interesting. I thought to put it down as psychological education.

I didn't see any Degas monotypes. Didn't expect to.

I left maybe half-way through the sale, crossed to the beach side, dodging cars, then wandered along in the direction of home via St Jean-Cap-Ferrat—a yacht club with shops.

I hadn't noticed the dogs before. But there was Cary doing the rounds and a pair of Great Danes loping about right on the far side of the garden. White dogs with black spots they were, or was it black dogs with white spots?

Rebecca prepared toad-in-the-hole which we knife-and-forked into our mouths while knocking back around a litre of St Emilion which got to my brain. I don't have a head for red wine and it makes my nose run.

We ate in silence. I had the distinct feeling that Aunt had decided that Mother and Father had bred a dud. Country people think like that.

'Always,' they say, 'check a mother's jaw and feet before you marry the daughter.'

So I broke it. 'Aunt, the Degas . . . I know you've decided they're fakes.'

'They are fakes, Essington. I decided nothing. It was decided for me.'

'I talked to . . .'

'You've talked. Maybe I was wrong after all. Maybe you do need a bit more of my poor brother. The whole thing would talk itself out of existence, given the chance.' And then, as though a switch was thrown, she said, very quietly, 'There's puddy tonight, Essington, and I want you to guess what it is.'

'I'm sure I don't know.'

'Don't you even want a clue?'

'What sort of clue? You want to play a game?'

'Jam roly-poly.'

She held the stem of her glass in her hand and stared at the contents.

39

'If you can't play "what's for puddy", I'm sure you would have been right out of your depth with our smart young fellows of the Côte d'Azur.'

'I talked to Pagés.'

'Psh . . . Pagés. Nobody in their right mind would talk to Pagés. You don't actually talk to people like Pagés. Rather you tell them things. And if they answer back you get yourself a new Pagés.'

'And you've done that? Got a new one?'

'Exactly, Essington. That is what I have done.'

'But yesterday he seemed quite understanding.'

'Understanding is what I don't want. I understand one thing. Someone has my Degas and I'm going to get them back. I'm going to get them back, you're going to help me and that nice young Col Winter is going to do the bookwork.'

'I talked to the valuer too.'

'Oh, I'll bet you did. A right little tart, that one, cross to kiss and all.'

Whoosh, down went the contents of the glass and she had it full again before you could say 'Bingo custard' which is, I'll swear, what landed on the table at that instant. At the same time I realized that Aunt was not the old sweetie I had determined her to be. She was spoilt, perhaps even cruel. Making Rebecca present that kind of food was not a joke, it was not eccentricity . . . it was much more than that. It underscored servitude of a kind money could buy.

I had been bought in much the same way. And Winter, Renardo.

'And what did you talk about with our valuer, Essington? How old ladies are to be humoured I shouldn't wonder.'

'He has the botched film. They did have to take more shots.'

'Of course they had to take more shots. To put the forgeries into place. For the *encadrement*.'

'But you had them reframed?'

'That was later. You see, I took them to London. There's no doubt they're forgeries. I had them looked at there, in London, in Old Bond Street. It was there that I had it proved they were not my Degas.'

'Then why didn't you tell me? Why send me on a wild-goose chase?'

'Because I wanted you to start afresh, from the beginning.'

40

'Or the police. Why didn't you go to the police?'

'I did, and their expert advice was that I was deluded.'

'Then it's one person's word against another's. It's an impasse.'

'Nothing, Essington, is an impasse. Now eat up your jam roly-poly and I'll give you my letter of proof to take to bed. You never know, it might clear that colonial mind of yours.'

I rang Dr Col Winter the next day; we didn't speak but his secretary, working as an intermediary, arranged for me to be at a restaurant, Les Deux Visages, on the Quai Courbet, Villefranche, at one o'clock. 'Ask for Dr Winter's table.'

Then I caught the bus to Nice. I had extracted the addresses I required from Aunt without sign of interest or approval.

At an art materials shop on the Rue Pastorelli—it had been there a hundred years—I stood where Matisse and Dufy had once stood and made my purchases. Then, in an excellent bookshop up a side-street off the Avenue Jean Médecin, I spent a small fortune on a coffee-table book on the graphic works of Edgar Degas.

I got back in time to see Cary cruising his garden. Did he do anything else? I changed into my Feathers'-selected suit of stern cut and grabbed a ride with Renardo around to Villefranche.

Chapter 6

A request for Dr Winter and the waiter steered me in the direction of a table in the sun occupied by a woman in an emerald-green suit and knotted red silk scarf. Not the Col Winter of my dreams.

'Mr Holt?' A very slight French accent but she managed the 'h' like she was Dame Sybil Thorndike.

We were divided from the sea by a narrow cobbled street, with centre-line marked by potted geraniums. Tethered yachts and fishing boats bobbed, tied to the wharf where nets dried and old men tried their luck for squid.

Looking straight over the water I could see the pink Villa Rothschild on Cap Ferrat's skyline and further out, the light-house.

'Sorry, Dr Winter is delayed. I am Sophie Vaujour. We spoke this morning.'

'And yesterday. He's a busy man, our doctor.'

'Yes.'

'Well, as you know, I'm Essington Holt.' For reasons utterly beyond me we both stood, awkwardly—if someone as chic as Sophie could be thought awkward—and shook hands, intoning like a reply in the mass, 'Pleased to meet you.'

Maybe I should have tried the '*Je suis heureuse à faire votre connaissance.*' Like in my book of phrases.

Monaco cars dawdled past, hunting a park further down the quai—Rolls Royces and Jaguars mostly. I was looking about, trying to take it all in, to store it, memories to scramble in the nursing home.

'What would you like to drink, Mr Holt?'

'Why are you "Sophie" and I'm "Mr Holt"?'

She laughed. 'Business is business.'

'If this is business I'd love you to show me what you do for pleasure around here.'

'For pleasure, Mr Holt . . .' she paused a long time. 'For, pleasure we gamble.'

'For pleasure I wouldn't gamble with you. And it's Essington.'

'What is?'

'Me, I'm Essington.'

'But of course, I know that.'

'I'd feel more comfortable if you'd use it then.'

A waiter had been standing patient at our side taking care not to wreck the view.

'A Kir? Such a nice colour.'

'Why not?' Feathers would have approved.

We were getting along like a house on fire when the good Dr Winter leapt out of a passing taxi like he was Woody Allen's stuntman. His huge eyes rolled in the lenses hung on either side of his nose.

'Christ! What a day.' Laughing, panting, rubbing his hands on the pleats of buff summer trousers. Col was sporting the international Anglophile taking-it-easy-but-not-really look with brogues and reefer jacket of light cloth.

It seemed a bit silly as back-up to such an unraffish face.

'What have we ordered for me then?' He asked after introductions.

'We haven't ordered, just been drinking.' I was glad to have my gold card just in case the good doctor got a fish bone caught in his throat and was rushed off to hospital forgetting to pay the bill.

We were searching the menu, me doing dollar conversions with beating heart.

'How are we finding our aunt?'

Like Feathers, treating me as if I was a child. And Aunt, herself, with her jam pudding. Must be my soft brown eyes, I thought. I turned them on Sophie and was rewarded with a Romy Schneider smile that made up for all the humiliation.

This Winter, he was the sort of kid that at school I could tuck under my arm, run the field and score a try with. He had a nervous laughing manner as if someone had done that once and he had lived since in a state of semi-shock.

We skipped the bouillabaisse—Winter didn't have the time to spare—and went straight for the grilled fish of the day.

'It's always, just always, reliable. What I have in mind—I've a telex coming in at three from Sydney—is we eat and chat, work things out, then I'll leave you to finish off at your own speed with Sophie. But you mustn't keep her out after dark. Ha ha.'

Just like that, 'ha ha', no real mirth.

'If we've limited time then . . . do you mind?'

'You go right ahead, interrogate. Gerald Sparrow told me to expect as much.'

'Feathers.'

'What?'

'We call him Feathers.'

Dr Winter looked puzzled.

'Sparrow, feathers, I think I like it.' Sophie must have caught a phrase like that off the TV. That's the way, they say, to polish up language, watch TV for Christ's sake! I'd tried that already. I had a nice big German set in my room. I hadn't grasped one word, not one. But I'd seen a lot of people shot, tons of rubber left on the road.

'What are we going to drink then? Sorry to interrupt but time, you know, is the master. I won't have a thing. The telex, clear thoughts.' He patted his head with the flat of his hand. 'Price is no problem; this is your lunch, I want you to have fun.'

There it was again, like a conspiracy.

I looked down the list; a Chablis at 180 francs. I indicated with a finger and caught Sophie's approval.

'Good, good.' He '*garçon*-ed' the waiter. Nobody screams '*garçon*'. I had noticed that already despite the phrasebook.

'I'd like to ask you firstly about the insurance agent, Pagés. I expect you've spoken to him.'

'Took it all out of his hands yesterday.'

'And how did he react?'

'Ah, here we are. Ah, good. Yes. They're all the same, aren't they? That's right, thank you, here and there and there.' Food in place he looked at his watch. 'And how did he react? I see what you mean . . . react?'

'Yes.'

'Well, he didn't. Not at all. Just burst into French . . . couldn't understand a word.'

So Richards and Temple's agent couldn't handle the language.

'Sophie, did you speak with him at all?' I asked.

'No, Sophie didn't.'

She rolled her eyes into her head.

'La Galerie de la Renaissance?'

'Ah yes, the valuer. Very good reputation.'

'I'm glad you think so.'

'Who questions it?' Winter asked.

'I had the impression that Aunt was not so keen.'

'Your aunt is seventy. She knows what she knows.'

'So, what do you think about the pictures?'

'Law, business management, I know about these things.' He shrugged. 'Pictures? No!'

'So, why do you take over from Pagés? He didn't know about pictures either.'

'I'm a businessman. I do business. If your aunt, who is, I might add, a very fine woman . . . no, a great human being . . . I mean, what a great trans-cultural gesture . . . to get up, to give up all for love of France . . . and yet remain a true Australian lady of the old school . . . if she wants me then that's business.'

I lost track. My interest drifted to a bronzed man in a toupee that looked as though it was made of rope, renting out a paddle boat to an English couple off a Greek pleasure liner that had moored that morning. A little further out the 'greatest power on earth' was whipping the water to a lather with a helicopter coming to rest on the flight deck of United States Navy destroyer *John Rogers*. Must have been hell bringing the chopper home on to the small platform at the stern in a big sea, the ship riding up and down on the swell. In the harbour at Villefranche, no trouble. The sea was a mirror for the sky.

Like everybody, Col Winter was after business. That was the yardstick for everything. I liked business too, not that I got much. But I sensed that back somewhere behind the illusion of money there might be an older world, maybe even a dimensionless one. Col was part of Aunt's world, the world of big money. Who was the boy from the bush to reason why? The riddle of the Degas remained or was solved depending on your point of view.

It was clear that Aunt hadn't told Winter about the report of the

London expert. Last night I had been too sloshed to read it. This morning I had still felt disinclined. It remained a treat in store.

For leverage I switched the conversation to the intimate relationship that existed between myself and Feathers. Winter seemed to want to keep favour with Richards and Temple.

Master of avoidance, as soon as he deemed it polite, he was inside making arrangements with the management about the bill. A taxi pulled up. Effusive handshakes, requests that I give him a ring when he was a little less rushed, then off.

I could take vengeance through the open account left with the restaurant. I looked enquiringly at Sophie. 'Anything you want? You've got to keep me entertained.'

'So why don't I order another bottle of wine?'

'You're the native, you know the customs.'

Sophie ordered a half Côte de Nuit for the cheese.

A man rode up on a bicycle to entertain us, wearing a flowerpot on his head and playing a violin. He rode backwards, forwards, sitting on the handlebars, then the saddle. He never stopped playing.

The meal deteriorated into a tasting. Sophie came from Burgundy, Dijon, and was taking me on a wine tour of her province.

She told me about her life, I told her about mine. Predictable really.

We pecked each other's cheeks in the French manner before she headed back to beat office closing time in her little they're-all-the-same-with-different-names car, leaving a trace of exotic perfume in my nostrils.

A paranoic, later I asked myself if she might not really have been working all afternoon.

After dinner I watched TV Monte Carlo. It screens an English language film Wednesdays. It was Wednesday.

I wondered if it was always Hitchcock's *To Catch a Thief*. I was watching it from the inside, on Cap Ferrat. Surely Cary must have been watching too.

It was good timing because that was roughly how I planned to catch a forger, if there was one.

I read Grantley Simpson of Old Bond Street's report in bed.

They were definitely fakes, but for him it seemed they would have always been fakes. Though he had looked at them he knew them to be false for reasons of scholarship alone. They were not part of the known Degas *oeuvre*.

At breakfast, frustrated, I pushed Aunt on the history of the monotypes. She was reluctant to open up. I had to drag it out of her, the first sentence. After that there was no stopping.

'Degas was an old misogynist, as I hope you know. He lived, remote, in a man's world. He liked to play with children and with animals. He argued with men and enjoyed drawing women and horses.'

Aunt Eloise had Rebecca bring another pot of tea. She was going to show me a new aspect. This would need a lubrication of tannin.

'You have to understand, Essington, that women, as the subject of art, represented fertility; they've been beautiful possessions, they have been idealized because in reality they fall short of the mark. The one thing they seldom are is just women—the females of the species.

'That was Degas's great achievement. For him they were things, little animals, like we all are in reality. Would you like more toast? I love this meal, it always reminds me of Charleston Springs. We took it on the verandah, Mr Fabre and I, looking out over all that dry grass.

'Perhaps in one piece, the *Little Dancer of Fourteen*—the bronze—in her tutu, hands clasped behind her back; perhaps in that there is a hint of something more.

'To visit brothels was a part of life for the bourgeois gentleman of the day. They were entertaining, sex could be bought and you met your friends in the salon. Like going to the opera or the Jockey Club. It was Degas's pleasure to do little studies of this world—as a kind of artistic aside. Casual works, but perfect because nobody, none of his contemporaries, could draw like Degas, he was the master. Except, perhaps, Lautrec. Even he lacked the sense of monumentality that Degas could give to the quickest study.

'Like all art, once the maker is dead, the work changes character. It becomes an *oeuvre*. But it's not really like that at all. Some things stay in their natural world.

47

'My Degas stayed in their world right up to the time I bought them. He had given them to Madame Foissy who owned and managed a pleasure house, very discreetly, in a once-grand house on the Rue Payenne in the heart of old Paris, in the third *arrondissement*. When I came to France in 1953 I was introduced to Madame Foissy's son, Gilles, by a dealer who lived in the Place des Vosges, right next door to the house of that old rascal, Victor Hugo. Very enchanting square, the Place des Vosges.

'It's hard to imagine just how little money there was in Paris in those days. The war had a terrible effect on all Europe. Art was mainly bought by Americans. It was the cold war and a puritan time, particularly in America. Women's legs were, in themselves, considered a sensation.

'Old Gilles Foissy was the concierge of the grand house in the Rue Payenne—facing a rather nice little park. At that time, however, not what we would call a desirable area.

'I bought my Sisley from the dealer in the Place des Vosges and once that was all signed and sealed and because, I suspect, he thought me less of a lady than his American clients . . . I was never one to mince my words . . . as a favour he took me to meet this sad old man living in a poky room just inside the house's main door at the foot of the beeswaxed stairs.

'What he had to sell was a box of photographs, taken in the house's heyday. Oh, what a big box, naked women sitting about, men leaning on canes, and with it my six little monotypes. I wouldn't have been surprised if Degas had taken a lot of the shots. But you must remember that in the 1950s nobody wanted to believe that any of the great painters had worked from photographs.

'I didn't like the photographs very much—we belong to our time. They looked dirty, unattractive. I suppose I thought them pornographic but I bought the lot. Oh for, I can't really remember now, but a lot less than we'd got two years before for a bale of wool. And then I paid the dealer twenty per cent on top.

'I was always rather ashamed of the photographs—I would have hated anyone to discover them in my house—but I brought them here to Cap Ferrat, kept them in a drawer right up until the week before I married the Colonel. I became very worried what his reaction might be to this rogue's gallery of mine if he found them.

Unfortunately, Essington, we misrepresent ourselves to those with whom we will share our lives and once we make the lie we're stuck with it. So I burnt them. Of course, it's obvious, I burnt a whole part of Degas's photographic output.

'But you see now, don't you, why I know that my Degas are real. And why I want to find them. If for nothing else than for the memory of old Foissy who might, as a child, have had his head patted by the master's hand. Whose father might have been any one of those fat and shabby looking dandies who stood there among their naked and semi-naked women, staring at the camera.'

After breakfast I wrote a 'Miss you both, glad you're not here' letter to Annie, gave it to Renardo to post and went along the coast for my swim at Villefranche. The Greek liner had departed and been replaced by a gigantic Russian boat with provision for car-loading at the stern, a hybrid liner-ferry called some jumble of Cyrillic letters.

The Americans were again playing with a helicopter. Their presence was a strident one. In the morning at eight o'clock they played 'The Star Spangled Banner' and then the 'Marseillaise' like scratched records over a loud-speaker so that we could all feel warm about NATO.

There was a group of GIs lying on the beach getting very pink. One was waggling his toes in time to a Walkman's silent music. I lay down to smarten up my tan and then returned to the water for the swim home which I tended to perform as a style medley, fatigued by the outward journey.

As I approached the house Cary's dogs followed me inside his fence snarling and barking. Curious creatures: now you see or hear them, now you don't.

I rang Galerie de la Renaissance and asked for Jean-Pierre. He was out. I left a message for him to ring, that it was about wanting Cibachromes of the Degas.

I had thought earlier, while walking around to the Plage de Passable for my swim, that it was not hard to imagine Aunt Eloise plagued by guilt over the Degas photographs. She was no ordinary collector hunting for an inflation-proof haven; she loved the stuff. That love could explain her earlier, scatty indirectness.

49

I was still confused. What the hell did it matter as long as you liked the image? But she no longer liked the monotypes because they were not the ones she bought. She'd lost their history, even if they were perfect facsimiles. For her they weren't even that. Eyesight or no eyesight, she claimed details had changed.

On top of this was bloody Grantley Simpson who believed that nothing existed in the world if it was not in a catalogue. Or was that just what he wrote? Maybe it had been as clear as daylight to him that they were fakes—a kind of knowledge that does not go easily into words.

Or did he switch them? What a perfect opportunity . . . there he was, the expert . . .

The incentive? A market? I hadn't even got around to that. The old grey matter was aching enough already.

I trotted downstairs for a chat in sign language with Rebecca. I wanted a tour of the service section of the house, hoping to find a spare oven and an ancient laundry. I had gone to considerable lengths, preparing my questions, writing them out.

No amount of preparation would have sufficed on the language front. Instead, on the spot improvisation and the cook's infinite good nature won the day.

She led me across a shaded concrete yard separating the house from a row of single-storied quarters and storerooms. There were two disused ovens in a very clean and dusted, abandoned kitchen next door to a pre-electronic, machine-age washhouse—complete with mangle.

'*Je voudrais travailler ici pour quelques jours.*'

Rebecca shrugged, beckoned for me to follow her to the main house and took two keys from a numbered board behind the pantry door.

Chapter 7

I didn't learn much in my two attempts at art school but I had developed a bit of a line in horses while fulfilling Mother's bush dreams. When you're not getting kicked about in the yards or digging post holes or straining barbed wire, your average clean-cut young jackaroo, if he fails to get into leg wrestling with the daughter of the house, fills the long—the unbelievably long—hours drinking and messing about with horses.

I had passed my time drawing. Once, home for holidays, I took a trip out to Charleston Springs, introduced myself as a nephew of Mrs Fabre and stayed a week producing a painting of the house with which to indulge Mother. I gave the preliminary sketch to the new owners by way of payment for hospitality. I've seen spirited bidding for worse pictures even if I say so myself. At the Beaulieu Rotunda it would have looked a masterpiece.

But, at horses, I am the master. I did four years of them out in the bush. Once I did the rounds of trainers and owners with a folio, hoping to use painting for my bread and butter. You can lead a horse to water but you can't lead an owner to culture.

I got Aunt's permission to work in the Degas dressing-room, opened the shutters to let a little light in, set up a card table and off I went with my book and my plastic bag of materials.

I could draw horses in a hundred set positions with my eyes closed. Degas . . . how did he do it? From life, from knowledge and from the action study photographs that were the rage at that time.

All afternoon I copied and improvised around horse reproductions from my Degas book. The side of the house where I was working was close to Cary's garden fence. I did one sketch out the window, of the Great Danes resting, tired out from searching for a human to eat.

My only interruption was a telephone call; Jean-Pierre con-

51

firming my character judgement by ringing back.

He had rung the photographer who couldn't find the second lot of shots. Maybe he destroyed them after producing the prints for Lloyds. But if I didn't mind the shutter imperfection it would be no trouble to make Cibachromes. We arranged for him to drop the positives into FNAC, a processing depot on Avenue Jean Médecin. I would pick them up and then return the film to him.

He nearly dropped the phone when I told him the size . . . I wanted them big.

'They will cost . . . what is the saying?'

'An arm and a leg. How's your Marquet? I'll bet that would cost a football team.'

'Are you really interested?'

'I'm working away at it,' I lied. 'I'd need the provenance for a start.'

'I'll send that. It's Villa du Phare?'

'That's right, and thanks. Put the film docket in with the provenance.'

'Of course.'

Maybe my psychology wasn't so bad after all. On a winning streak I rang Sophie who could think of nothing better than taking me for a Sunday spin into the hills.

'Only, Essington, they have all been burnt. There were terrible fires last month.'

'Let's go anyway . . . charred trees will make me feel at home.'

I had quite a line-up of horse studies, but no Degas among them.

'Is it all right asking Renardo to do messages?'

'That's what he's paid for, Essington. Only I think it would be best to do it through me. Well, proper anyway. It makes things clear for him.'

'Never says anything, does he? Or is it just that I can't speak French?'

'Renardo and Rebecca came with the villa. When I bought it they were the caretakers.'

'Oh, they're married are they?'

'Married or something. You see, this is really more their home than mine. I expect they already anticipate life under another owner. Of course these days people are less understanding, they hurl the caretakers out.'

We were upstairs in the gallery. She led me on to a balcony where trees obscured the Villefranche beach.

'See, over there, just to the Beaulieu side of Villefranche, on the rocky point . . . you'd know it from your swims. You can just see a touch of pale ochre through the trees. That was owned by a Count somebody or other who never left the Île de France. A local fisherman and his wife—he was a Resistance hero—were caretakers since directly after the war. They lived like kings, had the whole place to themselves. Must be two or three acres of garden. A jungle, Essington, all overgrown and terribly romantic. They spent most of their days fishing off the rocks together.

'That was purchased by a British pop group; made their money, I understand, singing of romance and poverty, all that guff. First thing they did was throw the old couple out.

'No really, this is Rebecca and Renardo's home; I just pay the bills.'

When I got back from my swim there were four books of Degas's paintings and a thick volume of Muybridge action photographs of animals, still in their wrapping, sitting on my bed—Renardo's morning shopping trip to Nice.

I spent the afternoon working at drawings. With the additional material I had more opportunity to experiment with composition, a very important aspect of the master's work. I had a lot to learn and only the time of Aunt's patience with a disappointing nephew. I was acutely aware of the tragic side to a man in his forties eager as a child to please. Still immature, and Father died before reaching twenty-three. Had he, perhaps, been as much child as hero?

Out the back the oven was on its lowest setting with the door open. I was curing a lightweight paper of the same kind, I had been assured, as manufactured in the late nineteenth century. Three kinds of Le Franc Bourgeois printing ink were being force-dried on the paper. I wanted to see my results and then compare them with the fake, or not fake, Degas. The historic art supply shop in Nice had been a gold mine but I was working completely in the dark, no

53

documents to go by and not a clue of what Degas might, in reality, have used. The Le Franc Bourgeois seemed the wrong stuff, the labels didn't look traditional enough but they contained exotics such as lavender oil. Anyway, I was not going up against the unbelieving minds of experts in high towers like Grantley Simpson, but of my fellow mortals out for a fast buck.

By dinner I had done a nice enough drawing in ink on Perspex—it took the place of polished copper. I stuck a piece of paper behind it, held it to the window light. Not yet believable but getting there. The drawing would be only half of it. The next thing was the printing. Degas was a master of technique.

A drunken dinner, the telly, bed.

Admittedly they were having a drought, the worst for about ten years—they come in cycles in Europe as in Australia—but it was incredible, day after day of windless sunshine. Maybe I should have gone for the beach instead of the hills as background to my Sophie-escorted outing.

At eleven o'clock the Great Danes set up a terrible racket down in the front corner of Cary's garden, beside Aunt's radio-controlled gate. Sophie's was the first outside car since my arrival.

Aunt had been warned. Buttons were pushed, voices spoke into holes in the wall, the grill slid to one side and the sparkling nondescript little sedan spun up the drive. Security was high on the agenda. I had been drilled on arrival and issued with codes and a little electronic gadget with an orange button to press.

I was waiting at the door but, like a girl's first date, I had instructions that Aunt must be introduced before we pushed off.

'In case you crumple my flower.'

'Mr Holt! I wouldn't know where to find it.'

Aunt was sitting in state in the silence of a half-lit room.

'So you're Dr Winter's other half, so to speak.'

'At the office, Mrs Fabre, but really more a quarter or an eighth.'

'There's not so much to him that you could cut up.'

And then they lapsed into French without even an 'excuse me'.

I sat like a shag on a rock waiting for the inevitable cup of tea.

What would it be this time? There was such a repertoire, traditional and herbal.

Your French girl doesn't dress down for the weekend. Sophie looked as though she was about to step on to the catwalk at the more refined of the fashion parades. She was only a fraction more possible than those remote beauties in her bone, baggy, calf-length pants, loose-knitted silk navy top, flat blue shoes and, maybe inevitable, silk scarf. Smooth golden skin slid into the shade beneath her clothes. She crossed her legs, recrossed them. Set in this old lady's room she was a flower: renewal. Could Essington be so lucky?

'What was it all about?' I asked as we swung into the Boulevard Général de Gaulle. 'Was she asking for guarantees of your intentions?'

'I'm sure she knows you're safe.'

'I wish I wasn't.'

'She was more interested in Dr Winter. But obliquely, of course.'

'And you know where your loyalties lie.'

Sophie had done her homework. Maybe she took all international clients along the same route . . . eating on the quais, winding the narrow roads up to St Paul and Vence. The French love of their country is extreme and she seemed to share in it. Her commentary was genuinely enthusiastic as we passed what patches of olives, oranges, violets and roses had survived the fires and justifiably sad at the sight of the destruction.

We had lunch in a charming restaurant which we finished up sharing with a busload of Germans; serious people who examined the menu in detail and then shoved their heads back into tourist guides.

We plodded around Foundation Maeght, a gallery of modernist art established by the great Paris commercial gallery of the same name, and I got rather obviously bored by the collection—tricky and fundamentally empty, I thought. Most of the time I was trying to deflect the easy and expert guide monologue so that we could slip into a more intimate mode of conversation.

No go. Not with chic Sophie. I was just another amongst the hundreds of Winter's clients. So I asked her if she did this often.

'Not really. I've done it once before, I think. For an Englishman.
You have an exaggerated view of my work, I think. Mostly I type.
And you . . . do you just globe-trot?'

'No. Mostly I'm on my knees.' Those almond-shaped eyes
opened wide. 'Praying,' I said.

'To whom?'

'It's more a question of for what.'

'And what do you pray for, Essington?'

I grasped her hand. 'For you, right now.'

'Why? Do you think I'm in danger?'

'Only if the prayer is answered.'

We laughed.

We drove back hitting the sea at Cannes and then bumper to
bumper through magic names like Juan-les-Pins, Antibes, past
the *aéroport* to Nice and around on the Boulevard Princesse Grace
de Monaco behind Villefranche to Cap Ferrat.

Sophie had work to do.

'Even on Sunday?'

'Even on Sunday.'

Cheek pecking and off she shot.

I walked up the drive to the clamour of the Great Danes next
door.

Chapter 8

While devouring fish with a French touch—mountains of frites—I managed to ask Aunt about her French conversation with Sophie. Had they talked about the Degas monotypes?

'Not at all. It's not a habit of mine.'

'And Winter, has he seen the photos the valuers took?'

'I shouldn't expect so. There's no reason why he should.'

'But if you took the business away from Pagés?'

'It makes no difference. The insurance is still with Lloyds. I just changed the arrangements.'

'So Sophie's never seen the collection?'

'How could she? Hardly anyone's seen it. Villa du Phare is not really Victoria Station.'

'I'd noticed.'

'She's a beautiful girl.' She was picking away, working like a micro-technician with the silverware. 'I always look forward to fish but I've got a terrible fear of bones.'

Watching Jean Gabin shoot everyone in sight with his machine gun—a TV revival in scratched black and white—I thought about my day, about Sophie's beautiful animated face, about my inadequacies as a hopeful lover. On each replay I stuck on the freeze frame: an offhand remark of Sophie's. We were looking at a big canvas in the Foundation Maeght, blobs of colour smeared on a white canvas.

'Charlatans,' I said.

'But it's so spiritual, uplifting.'

'It's a trick.'

For an instant she was angry. Like a flash. I'd been dismissive of everything.

'What would you prefer? Women in a bordel, like beasts for sale?'

Where would she get an image like that? The first thing that surfaced. 'What would you prefer, a boring still life?' or 'What would you prefer, nymphs and satyrs?' But why describe the Degas? They are exceptions in the history of art, not the rule.

Each time I replayed the scene I tried to make the film roll on an instant. Had she bitten back on what she'd said? I regretted my comment terribly. It established an antagonism that lay beneath the surface of the day. Or had Sophie worried that I might catch on?

You're a little out of your depth in a foreign country. You don't know what means what. Maybe that's what travellers like about it.

Swimming across the bay I breaststroked in close to pay homage to the rocks where the Resistance hero had fished with his wife. From where I floated I could look straight up the now-tamed garden's lawn and get a full frontal of the house. One pair of shutters in the pseudo-Renaissance face were open. A green inflatable boat was resting upside-down on a platform made by levelling the rock off with concrete. There were steps and an iron rail into the sea. Tall, recently trimmed palms, like cardboard cut-outs, dotted the grass. The scene was wonderfully artificial, as in a film.

I went back to work on my horses. I was getting close to a plausible Degas. Once there, I would need to repeat the image again and again until I got full confidence in my touch. This without slipping into slickness and style. Degas's lines search for form, they are never easy-learned gestures. One of the hardest things to master was the miniaturization of the image. We tend to work big—even out in the bush the spiral-bound sketchbooks I used were four times the size of Aunt's monotypes.

Late in the afternoon I found a letter left on my bed. Jean-Pierre Thompson. He had enclosed the slip from the photo lab—the prints would be ready Thursday. And there was a thorough provenance of the Marquet. Out of an Aix-en-Provence collection, one Georges Pons, Notary, died 1951. Bought at auction by a dealer on the Rue du Faubourg St Honoré, sold to a dealer on the Rue de Seine on the Left Bank and then another dealer and then another. It's part of the fate of pictures to be passed from hand to hand with or without the exchange of fictitious sums of money. It's the way the market works, even, it seems, in the big time. Maybe particularly in the big time.

I wrote a long letter to Feathers and a short one to Sophie and then joined Aunt for drinks.

Life passed with a set routine until Thursday. Daily I got a little browner, fitter, more expert at monotypes.

Thursday morning I had Renardo drive me into Nice in the Citroën.

I picked up the Cibachromes and hunted the stalls of the market in the old town, nestling underneath the castle, where I picked up a couple of turn-of-the-century prints framed under glass. I took these trophies back to examine and to try the photos out on Aunt Eloise. Sure enough, there was a blur on the Cibachromes, a white smudge at the edge of each shot—the problem with the shutter— but otherwise the images were fine apart from a little shine from the picture glass.

So they had kept the monotypes in the frames for the photographs. That wiped one of the possible explanations and supported the idea that there had been no switch.

Aunt examined the photo prints with little interest. But at least she looked.

'And what do you think?' The size should have made it easier for her to see. I propped the first one up against the brass base of a table lamp. It was clearly lit by the falling light.

'Have you got them all?'

I put them up in turn.

'Very nice, Essington, I'm sure.'

'And are they forgeries?'

'Of course not. You said these were from the first visit.'

'Could you look very closely at the detail?'

I put them up again.

'I don't need to look at detail. It's all part of the whole, everything comes together. These are my Degas.'

Up in the dressing-room I laid the originals next to the prints and examined them carefully, following each line and mark from where it started to where it finished. I compared the striations of wipe marks, mottled textures produced in the printing. They seemed close to identical, though enlargement and reflections blurred the images.

So, what had I proved? That the photographs and the monotypes were alike? We knew that. That Aunt could see the photographs as her Degas? Was that just because they were big enough for her to see at all? Was there still a possibility that these, the ruined shots, were set up to be ruined? That this was the second film and not the first?

If I became satisfied how could I make Aunt satisfied? She had her London letter and she knew that the monotypes hanging in the dressing-room were fakes, whether they were or not.

For me they were definitely becoming the originals. Was my task psychological from now on? Did I have to convince this stubborn old woman that she had the genuine articles? An impossibility; Pagés had found that out the hard way.

And what about Sophie's chance remark?

I had learned to live with the idea of functioning with a slow mind, though I have mistrusted the motives of people who point it out. Slow it might be but I know, if I stick for long enough, I'll work things out. I'd worked this out and the answer was a non-answer . . . the whole thing was a balls-up.

The Cibachromes were great aides to making monotypes because of the enlargement, even though the focus was off and the colour balance wrong. Not that there was any colour; Aunt's Degas were black and white—a slightly bluish black. The Cibachromes tended to sepia. I tried to recall the tone of the black in Miles Jackson's Degas and wished that I had included a note on that in my letter to Feathers. Such a long way from Australia, about a sixteen-day mail turnaround. Maybe sophisticates like the good Dr Winter used the phone but me, I hated it . . . in calls I forgot my main intention. There was no hurry. The trick was to hang on here in paradise.

I worked away on a piece of Perspex which allowed me to examine the composition from the non-working side, so I could see it as it would be in print.

Two horses, jockeys up, with a general sense of rail-fence, skyline trees and cloud, all pressed into the tiny space. I had already learned from tests that the ink had to stay very thin. Where I scraped or rubbed it tended to pile up at the edges and then, under the pressure of the mangle in the washhouse, to ooze out into unsightly blobs. This problem was hard to avoid and any reworking to get rid of it took away from the direct and gestural nature of the image. To a degree it was a hit-and-miss problem; if not for Degas, for me. So, too, was the authenticity of the wipe marks and the stance of the horses. Degas managed to get his horses to lift up off their hooves; you can feel this upward muscular thrust when in front of one of his pictures, even in a book.

I had four pieces of Perspex so I could make four drawings before traipsing downstairs to print; to where the paper had been soaked and was now lying interleaved with dishcloths on a marble bench top. Lacking felt, I had made a wad of towels and blotting paper to soften the pressure of the mangle's rollers as the sandwich—Perspex, towelling, paper and chipboard base—passed through.

I had got reasonable results already but, as we say, today was the day.

It was hard for me to view the four finished prints as possible Degas. They lay side by side displaying their small differences and, in two, glaring faults in the printing. But the process of deception was not yet completed. And I could take heart from the snippet of knowledge I had already gleaned from my reading—of the seven hundred attributed Rembrandt paintings existing in the world in 1920 two hundred were still considered genuine: not debunked. A thing only becomes a forgery when viewed by an unbeliever. Think of the thousands of experts, professors, artists, museum curators, who stood enacting wonder and enchantment at the master's touch while the bogus five hundred Rembrandts hung on the hallowed walls of galleries—private and public.

If someone, anyone, wanted to believe in my Degas then it would be real. But I was searching for someone who could believe in it as a work of forgery.

The two prints I had purchased in Nice that morning not only provided plausible frames but were, together with Aunt's Degas, models of ageing. I had them lying face up in just enough water to wet the backing paper which then peeled off in one piece: a monument to the days before plastic glues. The glass I left age-marked; it was very convincing with irregularities in its surface. If this was a forger's life I loved it . . . I had found a *métier* at last, an absorbing craft. I even believed myself to be talented. For a couple of hundred dollars I would have taken a punt on my Degas.

The paper took a very long time to dry completely. During this time I managed a touch of foxing by laying it on top of dust-particle-sized iron filings. The brown stain was quite convincing. Once totally dry they went into the open-doored oven for twenty-four hours in an attempt to dry off the ink. While waiting on this process I hung about the house; I didn't want anybody bursting in on my work, recognizing it or undoing it. So I amused myself framing my study of Cary's Great Danes with their markings, black on white or white on black. It had kept on arresting my eye. A fresh little study which caught something of the dog's power. I did this job with care but without ageing the art. It was a chance to practise sticking the back paper into place with a glue made from rice flour. It could, with a stretch of the imagination, have been a minor nineteenth-century sketch; the signature was a scrawl and there was a date, '86: the year or one hundred years ago.

Tuesday morning I carried my little parcel down the road, past St Jean-Cap-Ferrat to Beaulieu and its rotunda, to the unremarkable auction. Bits and pieces were building up in the delivery room, pretty much the same motley collection I had seen on my last visit. A sale was planned for Friday; that gave plenty of time for news of my offering to get around. Used to dealing with Beaulieu's British colony—the apartment owners rather than Bedford residents—the chaps in print shirts and white trousers doing the bookwork made a gallant attempt at talking in my foreign language, but they were not fluent. This, I thought, was in my favour. In Australia someone like Miles Jackson or even his fat-cheeked sidekick would have seen straight through me. Here in France they couldn't read the signs. Both sides, them and me, were concentrating too hard on deciphering the noises we were making.

The horse picture went in, provenance the Foissy family, father and son, Paris and Lyon. I had purchased it at auction at the Hôtel Drouot in 1964.

My name, Mr E Holt. Spelt with an 'h'—I wrote it down. Boulevard de Suisse, Monte Carlo. He lifted his eyebrows at that. It gave the picture substance? Perhaps.

'But I'll do the contacting. I move about a lot. Business.'

'Reserve?'

'Seven hundred and fifty thousand francs.'

'*Oh lá lá, c'est trop.*'

'What's that?'

'This is a lot of money. This is too big for our auction. Too much. This is just little furnishings.'

'But it's the price. This is a valuable picture.'

'Then take it back to the Hôtel Drouot. It is wrong for us. Look.' He waved his hands about at the collection.

'You can try.'

'It's not useful to try. Nobody comes here with that kind of money.'

'This is where French money is.'

'Ah, we French are poor. Those prices, your price, they are for the Americans in Paris.'

'There aren't Americans in Paris because of the bombs. Try it anyway, I want to sell it.'

'It is not possible.'

I stared at him: Essington, you forgot about the price. He was perfectly right. Of course this was the wrong place.

'Is there a manager? I'd like to talk to someone about this.' That was what Aunt would have said, only without the question.

I was led through an adjoining room, up a set of stairs to a carved door. The guide knocked, we entered into the white light of the Mediterranean blazing through a semi-circle of floor to ceiling windows, bouncing off waxed parquetry flooring and the glass top protecting a Louis XIV reproduction desk.

God had placed himself against the light so he was a black shape framed in silver. I put my grubby-looking pictures on the desk while I was explained in French.

'Mr 'olt, Mr Pic.'

Pic for pictures, I could see it in lights. 'Holt,' I intoned, offering my hand. But he was already holding the Degas up to the light.

He put it down, took out a handkerchief and cleaned his hands.

I was pleased with that. I had worked on that feeling: the aged look.

'And there's the other one, the dogs. I can't make out the signature. It came out of the same collection, which was mostly Guys, Boudin . . . there might have been a few little Delacroixs.'

Did he understand me?

I hated the light, it was hard on the eyes; my pupils stayed closed to keep it out and I couldn't see the details of his face. What a weak bastard to need a trick like that.

He picked up the Degas again, ignoring my dogs, and looked at it some more.

Bugger it. The light blew a fuse. He was rude, arrogant, however smooth he thought he looked. I reached across, snatched the picture and started to wrap it up as I had brought it. A newspaper parcel with the Great Danes. 'Forget it, they're out of your league like I was told. Sorry to waste your time.'

I went back as I came. When I was climbing the outdoor steps from the sunken delivery room I saw a man at the top, smiling his most enchanting smile. He had just come down the steps from the Rotunda's grand entrance. This had to be Mr Silhouette, descended.

I'd scored a try. Now for the conversion.

'Mr Pic?'

He held out his hand in, as they say, 'friendship'. I let it levitate and stood there holding my parcel. Like horse-breaking, there's a moment to move and a moment to stand still. The thing is to work out when to do what.

Mr Pic was lean and tanned with thinning black hair cut as a short crew. He was very à la mode, double-breasted shiny silk suit, grey with a fine mid-brown stripe. Tight-cut coat, baggy front-pleat trousers pegged at the cuffs. I knew about these things; I had fought to stay out of them when being retogged by Feathers and friends. What natty little gold-buckle slip-ons. And fifteen-denier socks I could see poking out between pants end and open-cut shoes.

Essington was come face to face with a formidably dapper type of man.

'I am sorry I appeared curt back there but I was so taken by the quality of the picture. It is not usual to see such things.'

'So why not try it at auction?' I asked. 'It could be the start of something big.' We had walked back up his steps together, and were standing in front of big windows. 'You could ring around. Monaco. Nice.'

He must have had connections.

'We will talk about it.' He led me off along the promenade to a chichi coffee bar with an English menu. Toasted sandwiches, hot dogs, hamburgers.

'It's a delicate matter, a picture like this that you show me. This Degas. It is too expensive for us to handle and while I would not doubt your word, not for a moment Mr 'olt, it is not possible for me to put something like that up for sale without, how should I say, guarantees of authenticity.'

'It's got a history. I gave that already.'

'But how do I know the truth of that history? I have a reputation to sustain.'

'If there's a buyer they'll check it out, believe me. If they don't, they're crazy. It's the buyer's problem. Try it, Mr Pic. Why don't you try it?'

I was drinking a big milky *café crème*. He, the sophisticate, took a *café* in two gulps, fortified with two cubes of sugar.

Mr Pic was thinking. What was he thinking about?

In Australia the art world is a close-knit community. They talk about Art's universality but that's bullshit. There's just a little clique who've got it all sewn up. They make the market, set traps, then wait. Everybody knows what everybody else is doing. Must be the same the world over. Mr Pic, my friend Jean-Pierre Thompson and all his neighbours in the Rue de France, the Monaco dealers; one gets a picture then rings around to find a client. They split the commission. And Paris was not so far away, or London, or Cologne; Milan was just over the border.

As with a horse on the end of a rope, I let him think. It would be good for him.

Looking out the windows at the passing parade I began to wonder which of the ingredients of the English diet made them turn to fat and blotchy skin. The seaside French look in better nick.

'Of course I'd need a receipt,' I said. 'It wouldn't matter with the dogs; we could start at six hundred.'

Now he was examining me, trying to work me out.

'I'll be direct with you, Mr Pic.' I thought I'd help him out a little. 'I bought these pictures in 1964, I stuffed them in my hand luggage and took them home. I'm an Australian, I can show you my passport if you like.' I had to carry it everywhere because the police were making spot checks, trying to catch potential bombers.

'The Australian dollar has gone through the floor, otherwise I'd sell it there. But a picture like the horses is international currency. So I brought it back with me to sell. Seven hundred and fifty thousand francs is a lot of Australian dollars right now and you know and I know that it's really no trouble at all taking it home. Or I can buy a nice little apartment and retire. Retiring on the Riviera is an Australian dream.'

A bit of patter to keep him occupied. Psychology.

All the time Mr Pic looked as expressive as Geronimo.

'Another coffee, Mr 'olt?'

I glanced at my two-dollar-ninety plastic digital watch that would keep on changing numbers after I drowned at one hundred feet. 'Actually, I've got to skip. Should have been in Nice an hour ago.'

'I'll drive you. I've a lunch appointment.'

What a stupid thing to say. Now I had to think of somewhere plausible to be dropped in Nice. The galleries were out. I didn't want him to think I was just trying him out.

'You've got your pictures. I wouldn't advise you to carry them about. You could lose them.'

'You won't try them then? I'll tell you what. You come up with a genuine buyer and I'll get authentication. There's a Degas man in London, Old Bond Street. He's looked at the picture already, in 1964, when I bought it. You get a buyer and I'll guarantee a statement signed and sealed. Make that a condition of sale.'

The pictures stayed with Mr Pic. The Degas would be visible in the glass case behind the delivery desk in the viewing-room. The next sale was too soon. We would try the one after that. The dogs would go under the hammer Friday.

I got dropped outside the branch of the Paribas bank at the Place Masséna. I thought that sounded serious.

Chapter 9

I went to the sale on Friday. It was a much bigger affair than the previous one. Maybe an effect of the country settling back into business after the long civilized summer holiday.

Not much in the way of pictures but among the bric-à-brac was a wonderful collection of automata with a little pair of mechanical birds in a cage that pivoted their heads and tweeted exquisitely. At the other end of the aesthetic scale was an erotic mechanical sculpture which, when wound up, set a naked man surging up and down on top of a female companion.

There was a lot of animated bidding.

As if to prove himself not an automaton, Cary was there in his immaculate whites. Weirdly, he bought the little drawing of his dogs who were no doubt at that minute ripping a thief to pieces.

Cary wasn't Cary. Not close up. And neither was a platinum blonde in a pink slack suit Kim Novak.

Jean-Pierre Thompson spotted me in the crowd and came over when we had progressed to the clocks. 'Looking for Degas?'

'No,' I replied. 'Wouldn't mind finding one though. I don't think you look for that sort of thing. In a place like this you trip over it.' Suddenly I remembered. 'Oh my God! I'm sorry. I've still got your film. I will return it.'

'No problem. Did the Cibachromes come out all right?'

'Perfectly. I've been wasting everyone's time. They were identical to the pictures, but Aunt still won't believe it.'

'Ah well, after a long life we are entitled to believe what we will.'

'A very suspicious woman. I can't get any peace while she's like this. I really don't know what to do. By the way, there were three of you weren't there?'

'Just the photographer and me. We should get, what do you call it, danger money.'

'But wasn't there a typist?'

'Oh yes, of course, the first time.'

'And the typist, she works for you?'

'I can see I'm not in the clear yet, Mr 'olt.'

'In the clear? Of course you are. It's just that I need to find an explanation, she needs it; something to put her mind at rest.'

'I'm sorry. Oh, this is me. Excuse me.' He whipped away to follow the bidding on a Carpeauxesque bronze of dancing nymphs. He hadn't asked me about the Marquet.

After that he disappeared.

When I emerged, without a clue what the dogs had brought, I had an impression of being pointed out by one of a group of three. That's the sort of thing you think in a foreign country. I have heard travellers' tales. It's amazing the number with the common elements of being taken down, mistreated, how rude the people are, how bureaucratic the authorities.

I heard a girl once at a party entertaining the room with the tale of being carted to hospital in Greece after falling off a motor scooter and all the doctors could do was play with her breasts. Obviously a fantasy. That of a pink girl among dark men. Your mind goes funny away from home.

I returned feeling like a trapper, satisfied to have set my traps but with no rabbits in hand.

Sophie had rung. I thought she must have burnt my letter. Would I like lunch on Sunday? Yes, I would.

'Why not here, Essington? Why not invite her here?'

'Thank you Aunt, but, with respect, there are the birds and the bees. I'm a grown man and . . .'

'And you've got filthy ideas! Oh, I understand, don't you worry. What about my pictures? Or are you going to set up as a playboy at my expense?'

'No, I'm working on them, I promise.'

'So Rebecca tells me. Turning my house into a forger's den. Who are you trying to fool? I hope it's not me.'

'God no! I'm not sure really. I'm just trying to get people excited.'

'Perhaps I've underestimated you.'

I almost watered at the eyes. It's a lonely business being a middle-aged man.

'Thank you Aunt, that's the nicest thing anyone's said for ages.'
'Then we must have a drink, mustn't we?'

Being Saturday the Plage de Passable was well-populated by the time I walked around the Cap from the lighthouse.

I set out on my constitutional swim and was treading water off the point, looking up the lawn to the façade of the rock star's villa through the spaced palms, when a Zodiac—an inflated rubber boat with outboard—putted up very slowly, almost running me down. It described a circle and stopped, motor lifted and ticking over.

''Ow yer goen then?'

I was a bit pissed off by the intrusion.

There were a couple of bronzed, blond-haired, blue-eyed characters looking down at me. Both had a jumble of tattoos running up their arms. I mightn't have known it then but these were the kind of little thugs they breed in English towns.

''Ey you, I'm talkin' to you. 'Ow yer goen?'

I bobbed my head under, swam as far as I could underwater, surfaced and struck out for shore.

I slapped into the side of the boat as it passed in front.

I was trapped. There wasn't any way out: the most terrible feeling. What did they want? Of course, I'd heard about the hoodlums. But these guys were somehow crueller, I could see that. For them this was fun, lots of fun. Too much fun.

I was old Essington who, at school, had stuffed up the boxing championships two years running because the other elimination-round winners wouldn't get in the ring. They reckoned I used to go mad, out of control. And I was in the water, treading it.

'Wanted a bit of a word with you, Neptune.'

They seemed to find Neptune very funny. Jesus, they howled with laughter at Neptune.

I went under again, came up and swam like Johnny Weissmuller. I was aiming for a buoy a hopeless distance away between me and the shore. My head was pounding with frustrated aggression like a bull in a crush, but I wasn't in a crush.

Crack! I was hit with something in the middle of the back. They must have been cruising beside me. I knew the motor could cut me

69

in pieces. Again I trod water, confused, but the confusion forming into rage. I could see ropes forming handles all along the boat's side-floats. I could see that my attackers were completely at ease, masters of the situation.

'What'll we do wiv 'im, Steve? Drown a fucker?'

One butterfly stroke took me to the boat, the next and my arms were over the gunwale, one hand on a rope handle. A leg thrust, an upward push of my whole body, and I was among the bastards. One went straight over into the water. The other hit me with a paddle, got me on the side of the head, just before I caught him by the neck and smashed his face down on the plywood transom.

Steve was splashing about in the water, slowed down by his trousers. Or was it Steve with blood running down his temple, blinking? I cupped a hand behind his head, smashed his nose in, leapt into the water and struck out for the beach filled with a kind of ecstatic energy. The Old Essington. In the boy, the man.

On the beach families were playing water games, lounging in the sun, smearing oil on one another. Me, I lay down, trembling; it was a while before I became aware of a sore back and a bruised hand. And then I noticed blood oozing on to the forearm on which I had laid my head. I must have been a curious sight on a holiday beach. Unchic, bleeding.

Self-conscious and out of place I trotted back into the water, ashamed of my blood. I swam slowly, painfully, back to the Plage de Passable. There was a Zodiac bobbing at the bottom of the rock star's garden and two figures were helping one another up the steps making a lot of use of the iron rail.

I told Aunt that I had hit my head diving, then spent the rest of the day watching TV: the international volleyball championships where France went down to Bulgaria, nine-fifteen.

Chapter 10

With the aid of a hand mirror I subjected the Holt body to a pre-breakfast examination. There was a long mark across my back, red around the edges turning blue in the middle. If it hadn't been for my share of evening drinks I might have had trouble sleeping. Any movement of the torso was painful. My head was sore to the touch; the bleeding had been from a cut above the hair-line; it didn't show. Maybe I was a little swollen above the eye. Otherwise an unmarked colonial boy.

As defence against another memory lapse I scrawled a note to Jean-Pierre Thompson to be packed with the transparencies in an envelope.

The film had been snipped either side of the six shots. There was half each of two additional frames. I hadn't bothered to look at these before, having concentrated on the Cibachromes. I held it up to the light out of interest and looked at the images. One of the halved shots seemed to be of the six Degas as a group on the wall. The other was a random shot of the dressing-room—a photo light, and between that and the window, a girl standing. She was blurred because the shutter problem had affected that side of the frame. The typist? So it was the result of the first visit. But wasn't it Sophie? It was impossible to tell for sure, maybe it was association.

I cut this frame off neatly, packed up my letter and joined Aunt Eloise for breakfast.

'You certainly did hit a rock, didn't you, Essington? That's not so easy to do round here. Lucky you didn't break your neck.'

'Not really diving, Aunt. More duck diving . . . off the point . . . a wave caught me and I crashed.' I sounded like a naughty implausible boy.

'If you're going to keep swimming you should get a crash helmet . . . This girl is coming to take you out? Very different from my day, I can assure you.'

I spent the morning in the garden, the pain in my back a constant reminder of yesterday's attack. Unless you join a street gang you don't get any of that sort of thing in normal city life. At school, yes. Even in the bush, in outback pubs near closing, the occasional fight can develop, though it's pretty rare, despite the stories. Me, I hadn't really fought anybody since school—a quarter of a century ago. There I was pacing the garden as though it was a playing field and going over and over the action in my mind.

The more I considered that attack, the more convinced I was that I had let them off too lightly. I'm not quite sure what I felt, just a vague longing to crush, to destroy. Scene after scene of revenge fantasy flickered in my mind; maybe a kind of insanity.

Aunt was off for one of her day-excursions into the hills.

The Bentley Continental was a beautiful thing—limited edition with a sloper back, painted a pale yellow—the ultimate indulgence I should have thought. Yet for Australian woolgrowers who had known the Korean War period nothing was out of reach: Rolls Royces were driven around the paddocks in those halcyon days.

I watched Renardo drive off with Aunt perched in the back.

Cary watched too, standing at the top of grand steps leading to the columns of his portico. Maybe he was watching me as well. I thought I caught him in the act. The Great Danes were not in view; sometimes I was conscious of them, sometimes they went unseen for a couple of days.

Sophie Vaujour was smiles and lovely to see you, Essington. But was it lovely to see you, Sophie? I wasn't sure at all.

'Sophie?'

She looked at me while skimming the edge where the coast road dropped into smooth sea.

'Do you know anything about my aunt's pictures?'

'Should I?'

'It's why I'm here. She asked me to visit because she was worried.'

'About pictures?'

'I thought perhaps she might have talked to your boss about them.'

'Nobody would tell me.'

'But you'd know, wouldn't you? It's not a big office, just the two of you.'

'I do the typing.'

'Then you'd know!'

Driving on the Corniche Inférieure, we'd just come through the tunnel on the Italian side of Beaulieu; there was a lookout on the road, no more than an extra car width. Sophie pulled over.

'I'm not an industrial spy,' she said.

'No need to get upset.'

'I'm not upset. I don't want to waste a Sunday being cross-examined.'

'Am I cross-examining? I asked you a question.'

I got out of the car, poked my head back in. I grabbed her hand and rubbed her fingertips into my hair feeling the cut. 'Feel that!' I shouted at her. 'And look here!' I said, pointing to the swelling over my eye. I walked out in front of the car and lifted my shirt showing her the bruise.

'Yesterday two bastards tried to kill me. Nobody gives me a straight answer on anything. Your fucking Dr Winter pretends to run around like a chook with its head cut off. You! You describe Aunt's pictures and you've never seen them.'

I was screaming through the driver's window, our noses were almost touching. 'I've got a photograph of you taken inside Villa du Phare. And you don't know a thing. Well, you will. The whole lot of you. Just sit tight and wait for the action.'

You can't walk on the Corniche Inférieure. It was built for wheels before they invented feet. I crossed the road and set out back the way we came with cars trying to crush me against sheer rock on the uphill side. In France they don't seem to have any of the residual guilt felt by Australian motorists faced with a pedestrian—guilt at entering into uneven combat.

I was considering a direct physical attack against the next vehicle that came too close when one stopped. It was Sophie returned for a second go. Couldn't go back and tell the boss she'd lost me on the coast.

I was standing telling her what to do with herself as lines of cars stacked up, tooting, all the way back to San Remo.

73

She really seemed put out, even concerned. Maybe I looked pretty pathetic. The bad-tempered boy against the world. What with the horns and the reality of the road and a sense of being absurd, I got in. I was feeling that more and more: those smooth movie people and big ugly me trundling among them as though I had just been thawed out of the ice.

I said nothing. Sophie drove.

She didn't take the turn-off back into Cap Ferrat.

'Just drop me off at Villefranche and I'll walk.'

She had a determined look on her face and the Romy Schneider glint had gone out of her eye. She was thinking deep continental thoughts. Whatever they might be.

She returned to Villefranche and wound her way to the quai, crawling along, hunting a park.

'Just here'll be fine.'

'Don't be like that, Essington. We arranged to have lunch.'

'To keep me amused?'

'*Merde!*'

We parked under trees at the far end of the beach. We had a long silent walk back; she was strutting along, click-clicking on high-heeled shoes. Me feeling more and more foolish, but angry still, and sore. A baited bear.

There was a table at our third try, Le Bateau-pêcheur, a cross between an up-market restaurant and a pizza house, but set on the quai where you might expect a certain loss of quality in exchange for the aquatic view.

To compensate for my silence she set to explaining the menu.

'I'm not out of the trees. We actually have places like these in Sydney, would you believe? Only the food's fresh.'

'This is fun.'

'I like to entertain. Look, Sophie, when I first saw you just along there, when you met me at lunch, introduced yourself, I couldn't get over how beautiful you were. With Winter, you were beauty and the beast. Now you sit there really trying. I can see you trying. I ask myself . . . why is she trying? And then all I see is Winter and Pagés and Thompson and a man—he's probably your uncle—called Pic. Remember Pic? He used to jiggle you on his knee when you were a baby. Then these two crazy thugs who tried to drown me.

No questions answered! You've got to see it: you become Spider-woman.'

Funny thing, I wasn't shocking her; she wasn't wincing. She was watching me, her eyes screwed up as though she was rethinking.

Rethinking what?

I wanted an avocado salad, that way they couldn't poison me.

'Nothing more?'

'That's fine, an avocado salad.'

Sophie ordered calamari.

'Calamari! We play quoits with calamari in Sydney. Calamari went out when we took to Chardonnay baths.'

She smiled a grim little smile.

'I'm waiting.'

'Waiting for what, Essington?'

'For you to answer my questions.'

She just sat there, fiddling with a piece of bread.

The wine came. I tasted it. 'Tell him to try again . . . it's warm.'

They argued for a moment in French.

'He says it's fine, that it is correct.'

'It's not, you know.' I got up, started to pull on my lovely powder-blue jacket. 'He hasn't even tried it,' I growled.

Sophie tasted the wine. '*Oui, c'est tiède.*' She spoke some more to the waiter. He retreated. But I was off.

When I looked over my shoulder I saw him returning with another movie fake—gold chain and brown chest, rope soles, blow wave. '*Monsieur! Monsieur!*'

Sophie ran across and dragged me back.

'Tell him to apologize. I want to see that bottle poured down the sink and the top label on the list arrive . . . silver bucket . . . temperature just so.'

Sophie started to explain.

'And tell him civilization begins with courtesy to strangers.'

I had the bastards running.

Mr Open Shirt was shaking my hand, sitting me down. He was sorry. Anything I like . . . I name it and he fetches it. No problems. Or I guess that's what he was saying.

'And we keep the same waiter . . . and he keeps on smiling.'

Sophie rolled her eyes back. She had done that before.

I sat down again.

Sipping a *grand cru* champagne, I felt like I was at an Australian picnic. 'Why do you put up with me, with all this, if they haven't told you to?'

'Why did the owner?'

'Maybe he's Thompson's brother.'

'Or, like the Indians, we believe in madmen.'

'OK. But I had to make that point.'

'That you're the original wild man?'

'No.'

I put my hand into my top pocket, took out the envelope, opened it and passed Sophie the half-frame transparency. 'Have a good look at that. Then we can talk about work.'

Even Sophie . . . did she lose composure for a second?

'Who is that girl?'

Keep calm, Essington. You mustn't overdo it. 'Sophie, why don't you like the pictures of brothels? Where do you get to see them? In the Louvre perhaps, or the Musée des Beaux-Arts?'

She was thinking. I hope they were paying double-time. 'They are not nice. They are degrading.'

'Most probably are. But I've never seen any. Aunt's just got delicate landscapes, that sort of thing . . . forget it. You're like a brick wall.'

She batted her eyelids as though I didn't have her on the spot.

'Forget it,' I repeated. 'Regards to the chef.' And this time I was allowed to walk away.

Instant self-recrimination: of course, working for Winter she might have seen the photos of Aunt's collection sometime, somewhere. And this wasn't a human being I had been eating with; surely this was the full 'Girl Friday' with the total-loyalty switch in the 'on' position.

Walking along the big sweep of the bay, making sure not to tread on the cracks between the stones that formed the sea wall, I found myself thinking, with some shame, of Karen: my last one-night, two-night, any number of night's stand. Her touch was my last tender encounter with the human race.

Chapter 11

Funny thing, once I lay on my back in my room looking out through the window doors on to the balcony and the Matisse landscape, I was filled with doubt. What if Sophie's had been an innocent remark? It was perfectly possible that her mind worked like that: on one side abstraction, on the other meat-market art. And there was an ambiguity about the girl in the photo. I held it up to the light. If I looked for long enough it stopped being a girl altogether.

Well, if I was wrong she'd certainly learnt a lesson about the *Pacifique Sud* where the wild men are.

And there was the impossibility of her not knowing about the business that Winter handled. Of course, he paid her. Why should she pass their secrets on to me? Why should she invite me to lunch?

Aunt returned, we got plastered and then I set off to deal out a little punishment.

I walked along the cape and took the dead-end that followed the railway towards Villefranche. A late train, Italy-bound, went trundling by; heads glued to the windows to view the tranquil sea under the light of the half-moon. I was passing the road entrances of a row of desirable residences, each possessing a desirable waterfront. High walls and iron gates protected them from the riff-raff and the occasional class revolutionary. It was in this line of houses that the rock star had made his real estate investment. What had happened to the displaced Resistance hero? The dead ones got name plaques outside their houses but those with the misfortune to grow old. . . ?

Where the road ended there was a set of steps down to the beach. I had walked this way several times before. Those steps gave on to a level gravel area reserved for boules; that was where the old men gathered. Now the only people were lovers in cars and a small circle at the beach's end strumming guitars and singing North African melodies.

It was not easy getting around the rocks. I guess that's why it was such prime real estate; but I got there, wet shoes and all. The Zodiac, pulled up, lay like an aquatic monster come up for air, glistening under the moon. I slit the floats with my pocket knife, memento of rural days—not one of your Swiss-army portable kitchen drawers, just one German steel blade sharpened down in time to half its width. The motor was lying beside the boat—the bastards were too lazy to carry it to the house. I took that to the steps and lowered it into the lapping sea. Bubbles came out of the fuel tank as it went under

I had no trouble finding a rock the size of a tennis ball to carry to the house.

As on previous days one set of shutters was open; there was the flickering light of a television set illuminating the room.

I walked on to the terrace and watched through the window: two lounging figures drinking beer out of bottles; them and the telly.

I hurled the rock then rushed to the shade at the side of the house.

'Fucken 'ell! Wot was that?' Steve and not-Steve ran out. There was an explosion that nearly lifted me out of my skin. The sky was filled with coloured lights. Rockets shooting from the Citadel across the bay. A celebration. Another rocket—more spectacular— then another. There was something special on, though Christ knew what—green lights, red lights, showers of descending sparks.

I was elated in the shadows of that beautiful night.

'Couldn't 'ave been that. Not from over there.'

'Take a look-see, Steve.'

He came around the corner. He saw me just before I hit him. The blow jackknifed him into my knee which caught him in the face. He straightened up. Stepping back, I clubbed him on the side of the head. He dropped. I kicked him in the throat.

Not–Steve looked like an invader from outer space: nose set and held with sticking plaster across his cheeks.

'Bloody 'ell.' He ran out towards the palms. I caught him, brought him to the ground, kneeing him in the balls on the way down.

You keep on going and you never think, that's the way you do it. They can't stop you. I dragged an unconscious not–Steve over to the groaning Steve. I'd forgotten my back, my head, civilization. What the hell was civilization? What those thugs had started, I'd finish. They'd never do anyone again.

I stood over them. Blood pulsed as a final huge burst of fireworks lit the sky. Steve was looking up, blinking. 'What cha want? What cha think yer doing?'

I lifted him up, carried him to the wall of the house, held him against it. He was a feather. Out there on the stations we had dropped steers twice his weight, one after the other, hundreds in a day.

'It's Neptune, Steve, remember? King of the deep.' I could still hear the mocking voices. ' "What'll we do wiv 'im, Steve? Drown a fucker?" ' I mimicked.

Then I cracked his head back against the wall, to keep it hurting.

'Remember . . . you wanted to know how I was going? I'm going fine, Steve. How're you going yourself?'

He shook his head. 'Christ!'

Not–Steve had started to crawl. I dropped Steve and kicked the crawler in the ribs. He dropped flat to the ground.

'Steve.' He looked at me with his hard little eyes. 'We're going to do this all night.'

'Oh, Jesus.'

I hit him in the stomach.

He sobbed. Would you believe it? I actually heard him sob.

'One of you hit me with a paddle, Steve. Was it you, mate?'

He was vomiting as he shook his head.

'Because, Steve, whoever it was, I'm going to beat him to death.'

'Oh, Christ! Let me alone . . . lemme go.'

'Not a chance, cobber. Would you have let me alone? Course not, you were going to drown me, remember?'

'We wasn't, no we wasn't. Jesus! I promise we wasn't.'

'What were you going to do then?'

'Just wanted ta scare youse . . . that's all. Give youse a bit of a fright.'

Not–Steve was crawling again. I grabbed his nose plaster, ripped it hard to one side. He screamed.

'Please . . . Please, just let us alone.'

'No Steve, not a chance. Not a cruel bastard like you. You've got to learn a lesson.'

The whole lot had to learn a lesson—Thompson, Pic, Sophie, Winter. It was going to be 'be sweet to Essington week' right over the Côte d'Azur.

'Why'd you want to scare me, Steve? You don't even know me.'

'They pointed youse out. Said if we waited at the beach, sooner or later you'd show. You were a swimmer, they says.'

So I was right. There was a 'they'. It wasn't just the old mind in foreign parts.

But Steve was calming down. It was not–Steve who was sobbing now. He was in real trouble healthwise, not–Steve.

'Steve, it was you with that paddle . . . I just know it was. I can feel it.' I grabbed his hands, started to bend them back. 'I'm going to break your fucking arms for that, Steve . . . for starters that is.'

'Please.' A long high wail of a plea.

'Then who is "they", Steve?'

'Oh shit.' And then he told me. Or that's what I thought.

They'd leave in the morning, he promised.

'Not in the morning, you won't. You'll leave tonight.'

'But where, where can we leave from?'

'From here, Steve, and quick or I'll kill you, I promise. You've got a car. I saw it through the gate. You just pop on up to Calais; you'll be there in about a day, and then you catch the boat.'

Not–Steve lay down in the back of their flashy Rover V8.

Steve was collected enough to work the gate's electronics. It closed behind me. Just before he planted his foot, Steve, to his discredit, said, 'I'll get you for this one day, Holt.'

So he knew my name. And he could say 'h'. Maybe a private school education.

I slept a long sleep of the innocent. Aunt had to send Rebecca up to have me come to breakfast.

'Late in, Essington? I hope you haven't been buying the favours of those Villefranche whores.'

'I didn't know there were any.'

'Oh, of course there are. The Colonel was always nipping over there after little satisfactions.'

'Doesn't look that kind of town.'

'It has to be, of course. Because of the fleet.'

We munched away for a while. Then I read from the paper which Renardo had brought in just as I was preparing escape. They seemed to have stopped the Paris bombings, for the moment at least. I ploughed through a long piece which fascinated the old woman, dealing with international talks on interest rates and currency values. Right over my head.

The Degas horses had had something of the effect I intended but I couldn't really understand what that was. I had got up several people's noses, one of whom I had never heard of, a Clyde Warner. He seemed to be the instigator of the attack, if Steve could be believed.

Obviously Mr Warner would get a report from Calais, unless my victims doubled back.

Upstairs, in the dressing-room, I had been playing around with imitations of the brothel pictures. Trying to master the human figure. Degas was pretty unforgiving eyewise, nothing escaped him and he had dismissed the idea of the classical nude. My figures tended to be a little bit too 'girlie'. I couldn't get the women to be the plump, short-legged but essentially human figures he depicted. Was he a misogynist after all? Or had he really loved his subjects for being just the way they were?

The mail brought a surprisingly quick reply from Feathers. Including a cutting from a colour weekly. I skimmed the cutting first and out of context. The grinning face of Miles Jackson was inset as a circle into an imaginative architectural perspective drawing of a new art gallery at Ayers Rock. Below this was a small plan showing the gallery's relationship to the Rock's two hotels, the up-market and the middle-market.

Not long ago a private university had been mooted for Queensland; justified by arguments about freedom of choice and the closed-shop conditions of the existing establishments. Jackson was making the same claims for this development. It would cost the people nothing, would add to the existing public galleries as a cultural service and could place emphasis in its collection where it was missing in the rest of Australia. Namely, late nineteenth-century European art and the art of the Aboriginal people of Australia and the Pacific Basin.

The plan had been developed several years ago and now had the go-ahead. The architects were named, a Japanese firm, and a fast-track timetable was given for the project. Miles Jackson was director. Bully for him.

Feathers' letter refuted the inferences and caustic comments I had made about Winter. 'Wonderful fellow, very reliable.' He detailed money matters: I was being provided for by Aunt the long way round, but it seemed to work; that was what mattered.

Yes, he had noted that Winter believed Aunt to be deluded. But art was not Winter's field.

He was pleased that I liked The Pelican—'a very special woman, Mrs Patterson'. He wanted me to keep in touch and I could always make use of Winter's telex. He would write to make that understood.

'We are, Essington, in the dying stages of the twentieth century. Whether you like it or not modern communication is here to stay. The letter remains as a literary device. "TELEX" is the word.'

I could see him pulling on the pigskin gloves, popping down to Botany Bay for a naive little wine from the Loire Valley.

Late in the afternoon I tried my first Degas bordel monotypes. One of them was really quite good. In the front the head and shoulders of a woman viewed from behind, head turned so that her facial features were in clear profile; with hair tied back she had that look of the heads of temple dancers in Egyptian wall-painting. Behind her, on a couch along the wall, a man, hands on his cane, dead centre. On either side two coarse, comic females, one wearing a slip, the other naked except for black stockings. The man was turning towards the woman in the slip.

It was really a composite picture made up of elements from Aunt's Degas and from reproductions in my book of graphic works.

My work had a certain vigour. The nice thing about forging was that you could measure the quality of the work against the original. So notions of value were not based on the workings of a

PR machine or on the social position of self-appointed experts. You could hold up your finished piece and say, 'Yes, this has captured something of the spirit of the master.' I had never felt so consumed by an activity before, unless, perhaps, on first arriving at Glencoe—a misnomered semi-arid cattle station in western Queensland—when I was given a bay colt to break. My horse. And I actually managed to do it.

Steve had said that there was a whole group of them . . . but maybe that had been to keep me happy. The only name I extracted was Clyde Warner.

I felt uncomfortable about my night of violence. I had fulfilled my desire; satisfied myself to a degree hard to believe. The old Essington turned sadist. Yet I couldn't deny the enjoyment. And since, I had felt unclean.

All I could feel now for Steve and not–Steve was pity, bastards that they were. For myself . . . I felt fear. What was I capable of? If one of the two had finished up dead would I have had a defence?

The auction room would be shut Monday but open Tuesday. I was looking forward to my money. Not for its value but as proof of competence in a new *métier*.

'Essington, are we getting anywhere?'

'Yes and no. But I think so.'

'I'm not sure that our mutual friend, Mr Sparrow, would agree.'

'I got a letter today, Aunt.'

'And so did I, Essington. You report no progress; Mr Sparrow couldn't report any either. This is not a holiday, you know. The red lights of Villefranche, splashing about in the water, drawing pictures.'

'Whatever you believe, Aunt, that is not the way I've been filling in my time.'

'Oh, and courting that Sophie; I should observe, without success.'

'You've hit the nail on the head there, Aunt Eloise. The typist: what did she look like exactly?'

'The typist?'

'You said there were two men and a typist—the valuers.'

'Oh, that girl. Just a chit of a girl. I didn't really bother to look.'

'But you were worried about the pictures. You must have worried about who was handling them. We observe people to see what we think.'

'Why should I have bothered, I was too upset. I just hated the whole thing and they were so . . . how should I say? I do remember the one who talked to me . . . persuasive, I'd give him that. By God, I wouldn't give him any more. They are a type, the men around here. You'll find that out, Essington. They are all front, there's nothing to them, nothing to them at all. Must be by the women who went on the game when the Sixth Fleet came in. Really the sort you'd think a pimp.'

That was Jean-Pierre Thompson in a nutshell. However, he'd been perfectly straight with me. Why had I lumped him in during my crazy Sunday of vengeance? Maybe the bit of me that had done that—the wild bit as Sophie called it—was also the bit capable of survival. Maybe it was right.

'The typist, Aunt, could it have been Sophie?'

'These young girls, they're all surface; interchangeable.'

'So it could have been Sophie?'

'I shouldn't have thought so. I would have recognized her. I can still see, you know.'

'In a different context, Sophie wearing glasses, perhaps?'

'I wouldn't think so. I'm not senile. I know who I'm dealing with.'

There she was, worried enough to bring me across the world, sacking insurance brokers, yet so locked into the careless behaviour patterns of Australian grazing families that she couldn't let on. Life, for Aunt, was mirrors and masks. I had seen the same women out on the station homesteads, surrounded by flies and the stink of skins drying by the meat-house, yet with haughty stares as though they were sealed on to the surface of the pages of *Country Life*.

'Anyway, Sophie who?'

'Vaujour, Aunt, her name's Vaujour.'

Watching her—her clever sparkling eyes, the superior smile playing on her lips—a new question entered my mind. Had Aunt stolen her own pictures? That was common enough in Australia—

steal them, or burn them, for insurance. Was I there simply to advertise her distress? Unlikely but . . .

You really do get screwy ideas in a foreign environment.

'Aunt?'

'Yes, Essington.'

'Renardo? I asked you about him before. But couldn't he maybe come into all this somewhere? He's inside the house, isn't he?'

'Essington, it's hard to know these things but let me attempt to tell you.'

I stiffened in my chair, clasping my hands between my knees, like I was hauled up before the headmaster.

'All this country—the area from here to the border—was Italian or rather part of the House of Savoy right up till 1860 when the people voted to become part of France. It was a playground for the rich, then as now. We foreigners, even the French from the north and west, we are a veneer. The ancient population is still intact if only semi-visible. They have a world, networks, interconnections. Humble servant that he is, Renardo is not without position in his own society. I certainly couldn't exist without him. He's a servant all right, but he chooses to be one . . . I sometimes suspect out of a sense of irony.

'They are honourable people. They can be trusted. One hundred per cent reliable. Renardo would not steal from me. He could not. There are depths to Renardo. Perhaps, one day, they will be revealed to you, Essington. Then you will understand what it is I am telling you.'

Chapter 12

I went through the Alpes Maritimes phone book, town by town. There was a Warner at Menton and one at Cap Ferrat. I was surprised, in among so many non-French names, to get such a low score. Neither sported the initial 'C'.

Not to worry, lots of people scramble given names. But then lots of people aren't in telephone books; people like temporary residents and holiday-makers who constitute a big proportion of the Côte d'Azur's population, and people like celebrities or criminals.

First time lucky.

'Mr Warner?'

'Yes.'

'Clyde Warner?'

'That's the one. Who am I speaking to, please?' A comfortable, slightly drawled American accent.

'My name is Holt.'

There could have been a catch of breath. 'Yes?'

'Er, you don't know me but we do have friends in common.'

'That so, Mr Holt?'

The name had stuck and he sounded a fraction chilly. But the mind plays tricks and I hated the telephone. How could I ever adjust to the telex? 'Steve, a charming young Englishman living round there on the Pointe Grasseuil, in a house called Villa Florida.'

'You've got me there. I'm sure I don't recall.'

'Oh, you will, Mr Warner.'

No answer.

'Mr Warner, I'm going to be washing clothes in the laundromat at the quai at St-Jean tonight, right on six. I want to see if they come clean.' I had rehearsed that line. I hung up.

'Who is this Mr Warner, Essington?' Aunt had snuck in behind me, eavesdropping.

'No idea, Aunt, but I should know in an hour or so. I'm sorry but I may be late for the aperitif.'

St Jean-Cap-Ferrat, a boat harbour with a rather nasty artificial beach at one end: the yacht club that grew. There's a row of shop-fronts facing the boats. Most have deteriorated into restaurants. How could so much food be eaten? There's a couple of second-hand boat dealers, a beach-wear shop, some take-away food, and smack in the middle of this a laundromat, *après*, I guess, Somerset Maugham.

I got there early, plonked a pile of rags into a machine activated by tokens bought out of yet another machine—they know how to sell machines—then set up shop, with beer at the adjacent coffee bar-cum-restaurant.

Right on six a tarnished silver-grey Maserati dating from when cars were cars pulled up. Two men got out. One was Cary, the other looked like he'd been called in to do violence. A stocky chap, not at all smart, with eyes flipping about the place like a rabbit sensing a shooter. Cary was in his white togs. The little man wore a coat.

They just stood either side of the car looking at the empty laundromat and the machine going round and round. I sucked the beer. When you're on a winning streak you just keep winning. I guess that's why they call it that.

A dark haired man about my size ran out of the restaurant two along from me, hopped into a Renault 5 and shot off past the Maserati and my callers. They leapt into the car and gave chase.

It was a short walk back to the lighthouse. I was in time for the ritual bottle of champagne. And getting to like it.

Aunt refrained from asking questions. Salmon kedgeree had come around again.

When I returned to my room Cary's lights were on. He had to know where I lived, everything led to here, even the drawing of the dogs. Had he bought that just for sentimental reasons? He had only to ask and Pic would have said that it came out of the same hands as the fake Degas. But the big question was, why should a rich smooth man like Cary ever even have to know, let alone care, that I existed?

I dialled his number and thought, before I finished, I heard another phone picked up—Aunt Eloise eavesdropping? No way out of that. This should at least let her know I was earning my keep.

'Warner?'

'Yes.' A silence.

'Why did you run away like that?'

'Like what?'

'There are a couple of things I think you should know. Your English gentlemen didn't go home for nothing. You know that, don't you? They tried to kill me and I hated it. Are you listening, because I'm serious. I hated it. And they said it was you who asked them. So let's talk, but without your little man. You behave yourself, I'll behave myself. You can trust me, Clyde, I'm not even a crook.'

'When?'

'How about now? Get it over with. You loop the Cap in your car. I'll hitch a ride. But just you, please.'

'OK.' He hung up.

'Hang up now, Aunt.'

She was shocked and respectful when I descended the stairs. And she was just a little drunk. 'That's not Mr Warner, our neighbour?'

'Not a word, Aunt, not a word. You just sit down and see if you can remember the typist's face.'

I could see the silver car head out the gate and wait while it shut behind. Then it took off in the direction of St Jean.

I walked the opposite way, towards Villefranche in the alternating illumination thrown by the lighthouse.

I walked till I came to a side-track leading down to the rocks, water and the pedestrian path to the Plage de Passable. A kind of escape route. I signalled the car as it approached, hoping I had the right one, and stepped back on to the track. The Maserati came to a stop, motor ticking over. The lighthouse wasn't much use, the beam went straight over the top of us, if anything increasing the sense of darkness.

'Clyde, get out of the car.'

'You'd have to be kidding.'

'Where's your little mate then?'

'He's not here.'

'How do I know?'

There was silence then he turned on the light inside the car and wound up his window.

I walked over and looked in through the back. It was a two-door but with a pair of half-seats behind. Empty. Nobody on board except Clyde. His window came down an inch. 'Am I alone?'

'Looks like it.'

'And what about you?'

'I'm amateur, I only hurt people who hurt me. You haven't done that yet. Not directly anyway.'

'Well, get in.'

And that's the way love begins.

You wouldn't believe it . . . the courtship took a while but there were no problems between Clyde and me.

I wasn't going back to the house, not with the dogs. 'Not that they'd be too much trouble. I thought about the dogs after the laundromat fiasco.'

'And?'

'Drop a noose over their heads from the fence, a choker. Easiest thing in the world. They'd cooperate.'

We had headed up to the middle road, a quick route to Menton on our side of the border. Clyde knew a café there. A good place to work things out. I went along with that. Only we'd change cafés at the last minute. He was too collected to be believed, right from the start. It didn't seem natural, rather something learned in acting school. Or at one of those places, like Scientology, where they teach the inadequate how to win.

This personality gave an artificial edge to conversation and to the car speed; we were going much too fast.

'Why do you need four dogs?'

'There are only two.'

'And your English friends?'

'Oh, yes, my English friends. They were to make you go home.'

'You like my drawing of the dogs?'

'Very nice . . . nice line, observation.'

'They were here before you knew I existed—the Steves.'

'What did you call them?'

'Steves—that was the name of one of them.'

'So, you just asked, "Steve, who do you work for?"'

'That's right. He said, "Why, old Clyde of course."'

'Of course.'

'Nice to know he was honest.'

We came hammering down into Menton where the *crème de la crème* once played and where now middle-class retirees paddle in the water. Clyde pulled up where there was a line of the expected restaurants at the foot of the old town. He must have had a favourite, full of friends.

'Not here, Clyde. Let's go down the other side. I liked the one we passed covered in neon lights. Made me feel homesick.'

Without apparent regret he backed out and we went to the place of my choice.

I'd reckon you could have bought a meat-pie at Libby's Bar.

'First thing you should realize, Mr Holt, is that you are not ahead.'

'How's that?'

'You're a forger . . . I could get you convicted, you know. That's the first thing. Second: what you did to our English friends. Don't think that it would take much to get them to put you behind bars. They are, to say the very least, resentful. You see, I've got a little more credit in this country than you. And I've done nothing wrong.'

'Then why the English gentlemen?'

'What's your first name, Holt?'

I told him the long-winded truth.

'All right, Essington, now you understand about yourself, about me and about the law. I guess, at least I hope, you're not the crazy you're made out to be. I'll tell you about it. Do you want to eat?'

'Not twice in a night. I'll have coffee.'

'Do you mind watching?'

'Go ahead.'

Clyde Warner ordered a hamburger and a beer. The waitress had a skirt that just covered her buttocks. She tottered about in white cowboy boots. She insisted on speaking English with maybe half a dozen words. We all turned red then blue then green in the neon light.

'I came here when I was eighteen; landed at St Raphaël, just along the coast. That was August 1944, eight o'clock, the fifteenth.

There were thousands of us. Just before the landing I said, "Clyde, if this wasn't war this would be paradise." You can't believe the light that lay over the coast on that summer day. You know, just beyond the beaches, the greatest painters of our time were tucking into a nice bourgeois breakfast, building strength for yet another hard day at the easel. Paradise, Essington.'

That was the man who had set the Steves on me.

'We went right on up, those of us who survived the landing. The French cleaned up behind. We went straight on to Grenoble and then across to block a German retreat along the Rhône. It's all history now. I was lucky, I survived. As soon as I was demobbed I took off for paradise. I had money, we were well off. I bought the house out there on the point. I swam, I took painting lessons. I was reinventing me.

'The more enterprising of us Americans saw the poverty of Europe as a signal, the perfect moment to put together an art collection. For reasons I don't understand, maybe because Hitler had hated it, there was a big push for modern art. The Impressionists were already big. Not just big . . . huge. I entered the market, firstly just for fun. As a joke. It was so easy. A little Modigliani and there was a year's income. I got better.'

The hamburger arrived, a perfect facsimile.

'I realized that the trick was to aim for the top of the market. Maybe every two years a masterpiece for a museum collection. A push-over. Canada started buying; Australia once or twice. And then, later, with the oil-price hike, the Arabs got going as well. And, Essington, I like it.'

'You're talking about fakes?'

'Fakes, yes, of course.'

'Jesus!'

Clyde Warner had just put into words what I had in mind. Only he'd done it.

'And you, Essington. Where do you fit in?'

Chapter 13

It was the umpteenth fine morning in a row. Looking out through the open windows over the trees and the sea I thought with wonder that such a landscape could ever be the scene of battle. Let alone on such a scale as that fought in 1944.

'Aunt, the typist?'

Renardo was enjoying an unnecessary washing of the Bentley. His mock humility was a small price to pay. Indulging the whims of a funny old Australian lady.

'The typist, Essington? I really couldn't say. Invite the girl for lunch and I'll take a closer look.'

'I think it's too late for that.'

'Oh! I am sorry.'

'Not to worry, Aunt. There's a lot of fish in the ocean.' I did not believe it, not really. Silly, perverse Essington. Very short on the old psychology when it came to women, or anything.

'Such a nice girl.'

I smiled and patted her hand. She really did seem concerned on my behalf. 'If I've lost the girl you might be close to getting the pictures. Anyway, I can always console myself with the commercial beauties of Villefranche.'

'Not to be recommended for a sweet young man like you.' Rising, she asked breezily, 'What's it today, swimming or drawing?'

'A bit of both,' I laughed. 'I'll change over when I'm tired.'

I walked down to Beaulieu's rotunda and picked up the money for the dogs—they had sold for the reserve—and set about extracting the Degas.

'Mr Pic, could I work it out with him perhaps?'

It was one thing to get a picture in the sale and another to get it out again.

I had to use a battering-ram.

Finally I got him.

'Mr 'olt.' Today he was in yellow linen trousers, full-cut as before, with a cotton jacket of a slightly washed-out emerald green. Quite a dresser, Mr Pic. But, I was assured, not a part of the world I had, until the previous night, come to hate.

No, he had failed to arouse interest. I sensed that his protestations against my removing the picture were more form than anything else. Eventually I emerged into the bright sun clutching my horses. A little disappointed not to have taken out the forger's prize but pleased to remove myself from the wanted list. I would leave that, for the moment at least, to the big league.

Then it was the arranged visit to Clyde Warner—would he be the same affable man still? In someone as self-contained as that, you could never know.

We did the remote-control gate communication after which I got all the way to the house without so much as a sniff of dog. So far so good.

Clyde opened the door. The sort of man whose presentation in everyday life is designed to make you wonder if you have food stains on your tie. I felt like a member of a lower species.

An Indo-Chinese house help brought orange juice out to a terrace from which we could look down on the one remaining United States battleship and the ever-changing flotilla of lesser vessels that work their way up and down Mediterranean shores.

We were hedging about our 'expose-all' night at Menton—that was expose everything but Aunt's Degas. I hadn't raised the subject yet. I gathered that Warner would know. If he didn't, as he was pretending, he must think that I was in France to muscle in on his domain.

The Indo-Chinese woman brought a whispered message and Clyde, with an 'excuse me', walked back into the house. I wandered over to the terrace balustrade, figuring that it would be better to be caught on my feet than sitting. Not that I had grounds for suspicion. My host seemed relaxed, even amused, when called away.

Then I saw why. He reappeared with Jean-Pierre Thompson who greeted me like a lost friend. 'We have been outplayed in our little tricks?'

'I wouldn't have thought that.' Looking over the balustrade to the garden I could see the dogs gambolling in their blood-chilling fashion; celebrating life.

'How's the Marquet going? Sold I guess.'

'Actually, yes.'

'There you go . . . My English friends never mentioned you. Not as honest as I thought they were.'

'Not at all, Essington. They didn't know Jean-Pierre. They worked for me.'

'But not just against me. Like I said, they were here before I let my fake Degas horses out of the bag.'

'That's right, they were here first.' And that seemed to be the end of the Steves as a diverting topic of conversation. We were standing around the table. Me, a little rough at the edges. I wondered how they saw me. If you're not the smoothie, you're not the smoothie; an observation worthy of Confucius.

So it wasn't just me that Warner was worried about. Something else had been going wrong.

'Pity, I liked the Marquet.' I said.

'It's sold; that's good business.'

More orange juice.

'Sorry, Essington, perhaps you'd like something stronger.'

'This is fine.' And it was. A change, a rest for the old internal organs. 'Jean-Pierre, Clyde, I'm still a confused boy. I've got more questions in my head than I can handle.'

'Then shoot!'

'Will I get the answers?'

'Give it a try,' tempted Clyde.

'OK.' I held up a hand full of fingers. Firstly the thumb; I pressed it with the other hand's index finger. 'Why tell me all this? I can't see how it helps you to advertise.'

Jean-Pierre looked to Clyde to furnish an answer.

'Well, there's nothing you can do. Knowing isn't going to help. Nobody'll believe you. Like I said last night, you've got zero credit here in France.'

'And elsewhere?'

'What can you do? Say to someone that some of their paintings are fake? They wouldn't even want to believe you. Then you'd have to be able to put your finger on exactly which ones and they would need someone good enough to prove it. No, telling you isn't a risk.'

'Not that I would have dreamed of telling you,' burst in Jean-Pierre. 'But what else could we have done?'

'You tried to kill me.'

'Essington,' Clyde intervened. 'We've talked about that. Either you believe me or we stop here. I told those guys to get you to leave, that was all. Last night you accepted that. Let's stick with it.'

'OK, OK.'

'Next question.'

'Jean-Pierre, you know why I'm here, you both do. Why not just put that right and forget everything.'

'We talked about that, Essington, that is true. We talked, Clyde and I.' Clyde seemed to be the leader. Follow the leader.

'Yes, we were working around to something when you put your horses into that auction at the rotunda. It was a nice little try, the Degas I mean. But I couldn't for the life of me work out why it was there. Wrong place!'

'Absolutely the wrong place,' echoed Jean-Pierre.

'But,' I said, 'it finished up the right place, didn't it?'

'I thought about that,' admitted Clyde. He must have studied film clips of Cary Grant. Or maybe Americans simply grow old like that. There was something boyish about him, yet controlled, smooth. No decoration, no gold chains, just elegance *au naturel*.

'That it was the right place?' I laughed. 'God loves the innocent.'

'Maybe he does. The only reason I saw it was because I make a habit of visiting the rotunda. For me, it can sometimes be a source of materials; it's part of my trade to visit there.'

'Question three: where are the Degas?'

'That's the question we are waiting for.'

'I'll bet you are.'

'It's more Jean-Pierre's question than mine. You've got to remember that Mrs Fabre is your aunt. Otherwise she is just another person in the world, just another one of us.'

'A man named Pagés wrote to the Galeric de la Renaissance wanting a valuation. A foolish little man. He was, I think, in love

95

with his computer. He would like it to eat the world.' Jean-Pierre shrugged. 'I saw the monotypes locked away in a little dressing-room. I could swear they had been in the same frames, lost in the same room for years. What you dream about, unknown master-pieces. Rare, they were rare. For me, the pictures in the house, I was staring at innocence.'

'And there were three of you?' I asked.

'Yes, three: myself, the photographer, a typist.'

'Who was the typist?'

'Just a girl from Nice. An English girl who does a bit of work. What is the term?'

'Part time. What's her name?'

'I can't tell you her name. Have you been hunting for her? She would think there was something . . .'

'Fishy.' Clyde assisted his friend.

'And she would have been right.' I concluded.

'Of course she would, Essington. We're all crooks, we've established that.'

I felt reluctant to fall too easily into Clyde's band of outlaws. But why fight? 'Could I put the question another way, Jean-Pierre? Was her name Sophie?'

'No, it was not Sophie. Are we going to go through the christening list?'

Then I was succumbing to self-nausea. 'Well, I wrecked that.'

'What?' asked Jean-Pierre. 'You wrecked what?'

'Never mind. And the photographer?'

'He works for us, but on contract.'

I pushed on despite the vivid image in my mind: the image of Sophie wronged. 'He knows there're forgeries involved?'

'Of course not,' cut in Clyde. 'We're not a corporation.'

'So it was you, Jean-Pierre, who took the first lot of photos of the Degas?'

'Correct.'

'And that's why you finished up with the transparencies?'

'Of course, Essington.'

It made sense. They had all piled in to shoot the collection for pedantic Pagés. Jean-Pierre kept the photographer ignorant of the Degas not allowing for the chance in a thousand that the shutter on his own camera would be faulty. Only the girl was in the dressing-room with him and she didn't count.

The idea had been simply to reproduce the works from the photos and then put them into circulation. It wasn't until confronted by the failed shots that they thought they could establish a situation where everybody could be happy. They hadn't allowed for Aunt's passionate love of the Degas in her collection.

In their plan a set of forgeries would be prepared for sale, a set made for Aunt and they would keep the rare works to put on the market in a few years' time, after Aunt's death. Against these they could claim Aunt's as being the fakes and they would be right. So easy. In ninety-nine cases out of a hundred they would have got away with it.

Jean-Pierre added, 'I wanted to own those things. They were the most intimate, the most personal works of a great French master.'

No one would have known the difference. And even if they had who was to say when the forgeries were created? I could see by the light in Clyde's eyes that for these two the whole process of forging was a work of art. Something like I had felt myself.

'The irony,' Clyde added, 'was that the return visit was a necessity. The photos were no good. Pagés would never have accepted them. So Jean-Pierre returned with the fakes already framed, identical frames, perfect. So, by the way, were the forgeries. How she managed to pick them I'll never know.'

'She loved them. And now she wants them back.'

'And if we can't supply them?' asked Jean-Pierre.

'Then I kamikaze into the whole mess, credit or no credit.' The great thing about the Steves was they made me believable. I was for everyone, unfortunately Sophie included, the primitive. To be handled with care. 'Dogs or no dogs.' I smiled at Clyde.

He shook his head from side to side. 'I surely hate to give them up.'

'You get your fakes back as a mememto. Tell me, have you sold the first lot, the ones you didn't dump next door?'

'Interesting you should ask. That's the other thing we wanted to talk to you about.'

'I think he knows that already,' chipped in Jean-Pierre. 'You told me you saw one. On a wall in Australia.'

'That's right, I did. And, I thought, maybe that's where they finished up. But why Australia?'

'We wanted to ask you the same question.' There they had me beat.

Chapter 14

I was sent home, a good boy, with the Degas, the six of them.

I worked all afternoon putting them into frames ready for the evening drink.

The old biddy recognized them immediately. She moved from image to image, almost with stealth. Maybe her eyes could focus when they wanted to, maybe long-sightedness is simply an expression of fatigue with the appearance of the world close up. The Impressionists were right, we all prefer coloured blobs in the end.

She poured a second glass, this time a Jacquard Rosé Brut, into the tall cut-crystal flutes, handed me mine, put a finger to her lips. 'A little secret, Essington. We must tell nobody.'

And I had hoped not to tell that the thief lived next door. It would have lowered her sense of neighbourhood.

'Friday, Essington, I'm having a little lunch. I was hoping you could join us.'

'That would be lovely, Aunt.'

'Just one or two old friends. Now that you've proved yourself to be, how should I say, acceptable.'

'You can't tell with us, can you Aunt?'

'To tell you the truth you can't tell with me either. Here, it took them years, years! With all my money. I suppose that's why I got stuck with the Colonel, rest his grasping soul.'

And then she returned to her wall of Degas, and she was perfectly right. They were the real thing.

'Your Mr Warner, he's our Mr Warner next door, isn't he?'

'He is, Aunt. I cannot tell a lie.'

'What a clever boy,' she kept on mumbling.

As advanced study in my new craft, I compared the originals with both copies and Cibachromes which were spread over the surfaces of the room's furniture. There were differences and they were all linked to observation and quality. You couldn't have seen them, perhaps, unless you had the originals at your elbow or unless you believed in the originals. I tried to reverse the relationship, to believe in the fakes, but it just wouldn't work.

I found it hard to believe that I had ever doubted Aunt at all. My own imitation Degas looked terribly lame by comparison. Back to the drawing-board, Essington.

I had outlived my purpose on the Côte d'Azur. My days of sunshine might be numbered. I wasn't game to broach the subject with Aunt.

Sitting on the balcony, watching Warner's dogs, an unanswered question sprang to mind. Who had pointed me out at the sale, identified me to the Steves? Why were they here in the first place?

'Clyde? Maybe I could drop the pictures off. Then the plate's clean.'

'Sure, when you want.'

'She knew them instantly, it was touching.'

'Great for her.'

'Here I come.'

I watched the dogs being called and locked away, then I walked to the gate and rang. It's a problem with possessions; protecting them kills over-the-fence ambience.

'OK;' fuzzy over the intercom. A click, and in I went just as the Bentley, Aunt in the rear, rolled down the drive.

I never really felt easy with the dogs. Not once I was in the garden. Even if you could shoot them or hang them or simply tie them up they were an unpredictable and menacing presence, like bulls in a stockyard.

Expressionless, the Indo-Chinese woman let me in and led me through to a tiled reception-room. Black and white tiles set as an illusion of cubes meeting cubes, slightly vertiginous.

I was relieved when Clyde strode in, as always in white, hale and hearty. I had been fighting fantasies since coming through the gate. He was looking more boyish than ever; there was a cream jumper loosely knotted around his shoulders. 'Sit down, Essington. A drink?'

'Great.'

'You name it.'

'Just a beer, that'd be fine.'

The help came in as if radio-controlled, took the order, departed. Funny, I'd initially thought Clyde an automaton as well.

'Here's the pictures.' I put them on a table at my elbow.

'Fine, fine.' Sort of impatient.

'And Clyde . . . I had a thought last night. There's one more thing. Who was it pointed me out?'

'What?'

'Pointed me out. You said the attack was to make me go home, remember?'

Almost absent-mindedly: 'Oh yes, I said that, didn't I.'

'You said it. Look, you mightn't give a stuff but I keep harking back to the guys who tried to do me in. Even Freud would forgive me for that.'

'Sure, Essington, sure.' I had raised my voice, searching for a bit of concentration on his part.

He half stood. 'Look, excuse me a moment, the dogs.' Then shot outside through glass doors and down off the terrace.

The drinks arrived. 'He's out seeing the puppies,' I explained as I guess you never should to servants. I got no reaction.

He came back in dusting his hands against each other, an exaggerated action. 'You were saying, Essington?'

'Nothing, just harping on about my death scene.'

'Yes, yes, important. Terrible . . . terrible mistake.'

'No mistake. Who pointed me out? Like they were at the sale. You were there, bought the dog picture. And Jean-Pierre, pretending he likes clocks.'

'That's right.'

'Then who was the man outside . . . pointing me out?'

'They didn't need you identified. I'd done that already, from this window.' He gestured across to the balcony outside my room. 'They could see you perfectly well from here. Most days I set my watch by you; out the gate, off for your swim.'

'So, Clyde, why was there a man outside the auction fingering me? But you're not interested, are you? We've fixed up the little mess and now it's piss off Essington.'

He spun around. 'That's not true at all,' he said. 'I don't know who your other man is, the one who pointed you out. Maybe it would help me if I did.'

'Why help you?'

'I told them to get you to go, sure; I said to scare you off. But no violence. Nothing out of control.'

He dropped on to the couch, head in hands.

'What?' I asked.

'Uh?'

'What's getting out of control?' I walked to the window. A car cruised slowly past on the Boulevard Général de Gaulle. Not unusual. I watched the dogs lope over the lawn.

Clyde was composed again, sipping his beer. The ageing war hero.

'What's out of control?' I repeated the question.

'Nothing really. The world.' He gestured large and sweeping. 'The whole damn thing. More confusing all the time.'

'You don't simplify it, duplicating things, forging.'

'No, I suppose not, Essington.'

'Who else put the Steves on to me?'

'Who else would want to?'

'Clyde . . . how about Jean-Pierre?'

'Hardly. I've got a feeling you let things run away with you.'

'Villa Florida?' I asked. 'Who owns the house where they were staying?'

'Who?'

'You know who I'm talking about.'

'It was sold, not so long ago, to a speculator.'

'How did the Steves get to live there . . . a palace?'

'He's a client of mine.'

'Poor bugger.'

'I suppose you could say that. He's happy. Lives in Chicago, loves it. Was looking for a caretaker. I was looking for somewhere for them to rent. A short-term solution.'

'Why not here? Stacks of room.'

'I couldn't have stood it, Essington. To tell the truth I was out of my depth.' The veneer was falling away. He looked plain depressed.

'So,' I said, 'you got a couple of heavies. What good were they from down there?'

'For when I went out. I'd got frightened.'

'You were fine the other night. And you had a back-up with you when you came around to the laundromat. Where'd you conjure him up from?'

'Antoine . . . he wouldn't harm a flea. A friend of Jean-Pierre's. Then, at Menton, I had you.'

'We were in danger?'

'I have been for months.'

'Who is out to get you, Clyde?'

'I can't say. If I knew I'd do something about it.'

You can't tell much from the roof of a car but I thought that the same one passed again. Bright red, looked American.

'Essington . . . somebody's putting pressure on me. They want forgeries on a contract basis. A fixed price. Altogether a different game. A repugnant one. Gross, I tell you their demand is gross.'

'You say no. It's the same as you said to me, Clyde. They have to find the forgery to prove you did it. Have they got anything else over you?'

'Not directly. I guess they're doing to me what I did to you.'

'Claiming they've got the credit?'

'Something like that,' he said.

'You ignore them, surely.'

'That's when the threats really started.'

'Why not Galerie de la Renaissance as well? Did they threaten Thompson?'

'He doesn't make the pictures.'

'How do they work? "Look Mr Warner, blah blah blah"?'

'No. Phone calls, demanding deals. Setting deadlines.'

'Deadlines?'

'Today's the first,' he said. 'First of many.'

'Maybe you're lucky the Steves went; sounds like they could have been moonlighting.'

'How's that?'

'Your friends also went for my rotunda Degas. It caught two different fish. Nothing small about Mr Pic's outfit.' Then I asked, 'You don't know where the threats came from?'

'Not a clue. If it's my talents they need there's no point carrying the threats out, is there?'

'Not if they think clearly,' I said.

Clyde grinned. 'And, in your experience, do people think . . . clearly?'

'I'm too muddleheaded to know.' We both laughed, breaking the tension.

The joys of forgery—I'd sensed them already—are in the scholarship, the finesse, making the history, finding the customer. Clyde Warner had talked of these joys in detail. Maybe a sale a year, or every second year. The telephone demands were for a steady output over a set period. Lots of works at predetermined prices. Or he would be put out of business altogether: exposed.

In other words a middleman was muscling in. To do that someone had to find out that the business existed in the first place.

Surely the only way was through Jean-Pierre Thompson.

It wasn't my problem. Except I got a nasty feeling that Clyde, in his tanned and remote way, was asking for help. I didn't feel inclined to give it. The old mind kept on flipping back to my swim under attack from the Zodiac. Probably property of Warner's Chicago-loving art collector.

Chapter 15

The instant I passed through the grill gate and before I could set about activating that of Aunt's villa, the red sedan, a Buick Skylark, had ground to a halt. In doing so it rolled me along the wall. The man in the back pointed a tiny pistol at me. 'Get in.'

I got in.

Renardo let us pass, waiting to turn. Aunt sat in the back of the Bentley with a friend in white. A couple of seconds too late, Renardo. I guess they didn't need to act films at Cap Ferrat, they just pointed the camera.

These men were new. The one behind the wheel could have been Dean Martin in his prime. The nasty little character with the gun had long hair spilling like a yellow mane over his shoulders and a face that would develop into a huge melanoma if he kept on getting that much sun. A slightly receding jaw gave him a rodent look. You could tell he was pleased.

And me, I was starting to go crazy again. I could feel it, a kind of madness oozing into the hole left in my mind once I emptied out the surprise.

The handgun was a small .22 affair, the sort of thing gangsters give their wives for a silver anniversary. Yellow-Hair kept it pointing at my middle where even if he shot a pin it was bound to hit something.

We were headed for Nice on the Boulevard Princesse Grace. Me starting to tremble. Nobody said nothing.

Oh well, stuff it!

There was a lot of stopping and starting; the traffic was thick. But if I got shot trying to leap out—in all that noise who would know? Who would care? The French don't actually fall over themselves to help foreign guests. Even the cops on all the corners couldn't make me feel like having a go. They were looking for bombers, not failed Australian art forgers with a .22 bullet lodged in the spleen.

I screamed as though I was in primal therapy. Annie would have been proud. I just screamed—Essington Pavarotti—so loud I couldn't hear Yellow-Hair tell me to shut up. I kept on, right over the top. In the car it was like getting lost inside a sousaphone. The driver was desperately trying to get through the bottleneck of the old port out on to the open stretch of the Promenade des Anglais.

'Shut 'im up.' More imported hoods.

Yellow-Hair punched me in the throat. Copping the blow I steered the gun forward; it fired into the front seat. I kept it going up till it smacked hard into his face.

The driver panicked; he took the next right, a street heading for the Place Garibaldi—one-way, the other way.

Yellow-Hair's head was going on the back shelf but he wouldn't let go the gun. He was glued to it. It shot again. I let him go butting his head as it came forward.

The gun arm weakened. I brought the weapon around so it was pushing into his stomach. His free arm was thrashing but not connecting. I was in too close,

'Fucken 'ell!' The driver leapt out and ran.

We were stuck, a truck had turned in behind out of a side-lane; there was a car in front, honking. It was going the right way.

I head-butted Yellow-Hair again . . . I got the gun.

It was an old area gone industrial—small, light industries. I reckon they'd seen everything. Nobody interfered as I let my Bohemian friend out and led him off along the street. 'Pardon, il est malade,' I mumbled in terrible French, arm around his shoulders, little gun pointing straight up his throat from under his jacket.

Behind us the orchestra had struck up a horn symphony—the only truly futuristic music.

What do you do with a damaged hit man on a sunny Tuesday afternoon in Nice? He was already starting to get frisky. His little mate was running the streets in circles—bound to bump into us at any moment.

I hailed a taxi. 'One move, I fucking kill you.' I shoved him in and across.

'Salopard,' objected the driver.

'He's sick, Monsieur. Rue de France, *très vite, s'il vous plâit.*
Galerie de la Renaissance . . . Drugs,' I added as explanation.
'English.

I got no reply. Maybe he hadn't understood a word. Yet we were
going in the right direction.

'I could shoot you now, Blondie, exit at the next corner. That
would be it. Nothing's stopping me. Didn't they tell you about the
last lot?'

No reply. Sulky. Vicious when winning, a coward in defeat.

We had to loop around, the streets all being one-way. A
stranger's nightmare.

I gave the driver two hundred francs. A lot of that to clean the
taxi of blood.

Blondie broke free, made a little canter down the street and
headed straight across for the Hotel Négresco; down along a side-
street to where it sat in pride facing the sun. I was gaining when he
hit the six lanes of the Promenade des Anglais. He was brought to
an abrupt halt by the stream of cars speeding bumper to bumper.
Just a moment's hesitation and then he was off. But the moment
was long enough for me to throw myself through the gap
separating us and bring him down, to the alarm of the two
elaborately costumed bell-boys who hovered outside the fabled
hotel's doors. I whipped him in through the gate of the next door
park before anyone had time to recover from the shock of what
they had seen. Once the garden of a grand villa, the raked gravel
paths led back to the Rue de France. Old couples sat on bright blue
benches, basking. Their dogs basked at their feet.

With the pistol pointing to God via my prisoner's head, I was
back in control. We walked through iron gates, the decorations of
which had been picked out with gilt, and headed over to Jean-
Pierre's establishment opposite.

As soon as we were in Thompson locked the door. In fright I
guess.

'Great,' I said, retreating to the dealer's desk near the only other
exit. I covered them both with the semi-toy gun—just in case.

'Essington!'

'Sorry about this, I'm all excited, can't think straight. You just
stay over there.'

He stepped forward.

I pointed the gun at his nose, tightened my grip.

He stopped. By touch I shut the door at my back; I turned the key then removed it. 'Now, very slow, walk to the phone. Yellow-Hair, you stick with him, close. All I want is for things to quiet down. We don't want to wreck all this junk.'

Only the thug knew how many bullets were in the gun. I felt I would be better rid of the thing. Nasty. I didn't like it at all.

'Pick the receiver up, Jean-Pierre. That's right. Hold it. Tell me Warner's number.'

'Nine-three-four-seven-six-one-two-seven.'

'You sure? You don't need to look it up?'

He shook his head but you could see he was thinking.

'Then try it. Get it right. Remember anyone else you ring is too far away. Even the police.'

He dialled the eight numbers all in a row. Did they know one another, the thug and the dealer on the Rue de France? No sign.

'Clyde. He's here.' Jean-Pierre looked to me for guidance.

'Go on . . . tell him who.'

''olt's here . . . Essington 'olt. He is here at the gallery.'

'And tell him who else.'

'He's got some man with him.'

I couldn't tell if that made sense to Warner or not.

Yellow-Hair was looking fidgety. 'Knuckles,' I commanded, 'lie down on the floor. Slowly does it.' He went down. 'Flat on your face.'

There wasn't all that much space in the gallery. I didn't like the situation—an impasse. And it looked like I'd got it wrong. 'Tell him to come here quick.'

'Clyde,' said Jean-Pierre, 'he wants you to come to the gallery.'

Warner was saying something. 'Just drop it,' I said. 'Put the fucking thing down.' He did as he was told.

Then I asked: 'Well, Thompson, what's happening?'

'He said he'd come. But why, Essington? What is this about?'

'That's what we're going to find out. Or at least I hope so. Meantime it's going to be uncomfortable. I don't feel like trusting anyone. Don't move a muscle, Jean-Pierre; like that friend of yours.' I pointed to the figure on the floor.

'A friend of mine? I've never seen that man.'

'Blondie?' I asked.

'Don't ask me,' he mumbled into the carpet.

'You'll tell me everything in the end, cobber. Never mind about that.'

In the half-hour it took Warner to arrive I nearly went out of my mind. Half an hour of watching, waiting for unexpected movement, waiting for police or, worse, for more Yellow-Hairs to come ploughing through the street window.

I worked out in the old Essington Holt mind that if Warner arrived it proved something. But I couldn't see what.

Through the windows I watched him alight from a taxi—like 'take one' of a B-grade movie.

Yellow-Hair was still flat on his face and nursing a hand I trod on when he had made an unwise gesture. I was getting used to that sort of thing. Some people are late starters—arrested development. I could think of Churchill straight off. Greatness thrust upon him.

I still had to choose. I had discovered forgery and brute force all at the same moment. The Gods had been generous. 'Unlock the door, Jean-Pierre, and then step back.'

Warner entered.

'Shut it. That's nice. And lock it. Sorry, Clyde, just stay over there.'

'Essington, what do you think you're up to?'

I shook my head. 'I've got nothing to answer. Why don't you ask your old mate for the details or have a go at Blondie. He's out of the same stable as the Steves. He wants to kill me. Another one of yours, Clyde?'

He reached out towards me. 'Stop! I'm happy to kill any of you straight off. I'm just under control.' I waved the gun about. 'Start talking.'

'What can I talk about? There's nothing to say.' Clyde protested.

'Maybe Jean-Pierre'll give you a lead.'

The dealer blew air out between his lips—the pouting gesture of French disassociation.

'Blondie? Which one of these guys pays you?' I asked.

He lay still and quiet.

'Nothing,' I shouted. 'Fucking nothing! I walk out of your house this morning and there's a car waiting to hit me. Why was that Clyde?'

'I didn't put it there. Remember, you rang me.'

'And today was your deadline? Was I some kind of pay-off?'

He didn't answer my question.

'You told him about that?' Jean-Pierre turned on Warner, surprised.

'Maybe he could help. The first person I knew who had to be uninvolved.'

'And now he thinks it's me?'

'That's right, Jean-Pierre,' I said. 'I think you've got something to do with everything. You're the public face, the shop-front. Whatever works, works through you.'

Silence.

'I'll try the golden boy for answers then,' I said.

I sat him up on a delicate carved chair with a little hunting scene woven into the seat: falconers and pheasants and squires on horseback. I gestured for Jean-Pierre and Clyde to move behind him. 'No fucking about.'

Funny really, they weren't all that scared. I don't think Clyde was scared at all. An aesthete, I guess he just liked things to look good. And this looked bad.

I hit Blondie hard on the side of the face with the pistol. It was small but maybe the weight of a carpenter's hammer head.

'Who do you work for?' No answer. 'I'm going to do this all day.'

Not a word. I hit him again.

I could see Clyde wince at the blow. 'Tell him,' he said. 'He'll kill you if you don't. Take it from me. You're his second lot. Tell him kid, and I'll buy you a ticket to anywhere out of here and money for a couple of months. Let him think, Essington.'

I watched Jean-Pierre. He was staring at the long blond hair hanging down the back of the goon's neck.

'Money first?'

'Money and tickets at the airport, on delivery.'

'S'at a deal?'

110

'If you can deliver. Get your car, Jean-Pierre. Let him go, Essington.'

Clyde had what they used to call 'authority', when he wanted.

Blondie got his money and his tickets. We stayed with him till he went in through the gate. A sorry sight.

I was feeling sheepish; there was a teasing note when Clyde asked if I felt safe alone with them. 'Get your gun out if you like.' We pulled in outside the gallery, crossed over, walked down the side-road to the Negresco for a drink. I was in need of one.

'You said you saw the Degas monotype in Australia?' Jean-Pierre asked once we had settled down by a window looking out over the Promenade des Anglais to where the sea was really azure—like the coast's name.

'In Sydney.'

'Just one.'

'One, on a dealer's wall. So?'

A waiter approached with perfect discretion. Clyde ordered three whisky sours by mutual consent.

'They were Australians who bought them. Two men. One might have been working for the other. Maybe just the older man bought them.'

'Their names?'

'No names, just cash,' Jean-Pierre replied.

'And it's Australians paying to get people beaten up, so Yellow-Hair tells us.' I smiled, adding, 'We have a reputation to uphold.'

'I'll grant you that, Essington,' said Clyde. 'But what do they want?'

'What they've told you already over the phone.'

With Clyde and Jean-Pierre together it was like watching a pair of well-rehearsed actors going through their parts. I got the feeling I would never get at the truth. Not with them anyway. And yet they enchanted me, they could win me over any time at all.

'Why would they pay my price if they knew they were fakes?' Jean-Pierre asked. 'And in cash.'

'Because,' Clyde replied, 'they wanted to test them as fakes, try them out further down the line. They were just about to buy the forger, they had to test the product. Whatever the reason,'—he dropped his face into his hands—'I just want to keep out of this mess. I'd rather mass produce than slip down into this brutality.'

'That's why you agreed to go along with them?' I asked. 'They'll get worse. If they lean on you at the start what happens at the end?'

'I'll find that out, I guess.' He skolled his drink, held out a hand to Jean-Pierre. 'The end of a long and fruitful partnership. For the moment anyway.'

'So? Now you wait for another call?' asked the dealer.

'I wait.'

'And Essington?'

'I think I'll go and try out Yellow-Hair's contact. We Australians, we're a clubbish bunch.' The story we'd got on the way to the airport concerned the good Dr Winter. He had been the employer. Me, I wasn't a hundred per cent convinced; but where in hell had the name come from? It made sense and it didn't make sense. The bespectacled accountant didn't seem the type. More likely he'd been called in to act for a third party. And then there was Sophie. If the information was correct what did it make her?

'If he is the man and you talk to him, where does that leave my acceptance of the conditions?' Clyde demanded.

'I've thought of that. Anyway, there's lots of reasons for us to talk. We're compatriots. And I don't even know the Rugby League ladder.'

I was sipping my drink when Clyde ordered three more. It might have been an elegant room and the sea might have shone. Beautiful women may have promenaded up and down inside and out but I didn't care. The charms of the Côte d'Azur were fading. I was filled with a desire to go home to the *Pacifique Sud*.

And then a thought drifted in. What do they do with abandoned cars?

Answer. They tow them away. You pay a fortune to get them back.

And what had happened to the second hood, Yellow-Hair's mate?

As it turned out events caught up with me. What had passed that day became of little consequence; it was put on the back burner.

Chapter 16

Being daylight saving it was bright sunlight when I got back. Renardo and Rebecca looked grim when they opened the door together.

And then I saw Aunt's friend in white. She was an English nurse, all starched and clean. Really a bit of a blast from the past.

Renardo led me up to her as to a queen. 'Monsieur 'olt,' he said, and gestured, 'Madame 'ampton.'

'Hampton,' she said, and shook my hand. 'I'm afraid your aunt's not a well woman. I'm here to look after her.'

'But, this morning she . . .'

'It's nothing sudden, Mr Holt.' She assumed the 'h'. It's been with her quite a time now. The doctors have decided to call in Nurse Hampton. From now on she'll need constant nursing, Mr Holt. But she's in good hands, rest assured of that.'

'I'd like to see her,' I said.

'Certainly, you have only to ask.'

'She's here to watch me die, Essington. Isn't she wonderful, so big and overbearing. Just what I'd always thought a nurse should be.'

'But you're not going to die, Aunt.'

'Oh yes I am, Essington. Just as sure as pigs have little tails. Since well before you arrived. And we're not going to stop it. We can't. And anyway, why should we?

'I think she's perfectly wonderful. She makes me think of Wagner's Valkyries, only instead of a spear . . . I do love their spears, don't you? They always look so blunt on stage . . . only instead of a spear I expect she'll have a hypodermic syringe.'

'Oh, Aunt.' I clasped her hand and kissed her on the cheek.

She was sitting up—a doll—looking absolutely unkillable. 'For the death scenes, Essington, two rules: no sentimentality and no wowsers. Nurse Hampton is on a promise not to cut out the wine.

I've had a guarantee, you see. They are not easy to find, the Nurse Hamptons of this world. Nor are the Dr Morlinos.

'When I first had problems I followed the advice, the bad advice, of the British colony, and went over to London. That's when I had my Degas looked at, you see. Worthless, your Harley Street people. They pretend that they don't believe in death. What a terrible joke they all were. This therapy, that therapy. All I wanted was to know. So I could get ready, I suppose.

'But our Dr Morlino . . . you see, he's a Catholic, not by inclination but by tradition. No choice in it.'

I still held her hand. I could feel it, terribly small, a fledgling cupped between mine. I could feel the little gun in my pocket where it had jammed between me and the back of the chair.

I gave a shudder.

'I'm glad you're here, Essington, because we're going to have such fun you and me and our big strapping nurse, aren't we? And don't go forgetting Friday, will you?'

'Friday?'

'My lunch, Essington. We're not going to let a little clump of cells get in our way.'

We sat in silence. In the distance sounded the toot of a train hurrying from France to Italy or vice versa.

It had never been possible to share with Mother, to share in the sense of being human. Now this old woman, sister of my fabled father, was leading me into the human race.

We must have sat for quite a long time. Suddenly I was aware of fading light, then electric light, then Nurse Hampton.

'What a touching sight.' She stood, hands on ample hips. 'Still and all, we've got to shake a leg, haven't we, or we'll miss our dinner.'

'First lesson, nurse, is that I am not some kind of undifferentiated collective. I am singular as you will no doubt come to learn. A singular me rules this house. After all, what's the use of all those years if you can't at least feel the reality of your will?'

It was like a first discharge of rifles. Hampton's assault fell back leaving its dead and dying on the battlefield.

'About this time we take a little drink, don't we, Essington?'

'Indeed we do, Aunt.'

'Perhaps you'd like to join us, nurse. You'll find it clears the palate for the meal to come.'

'Thank you, Mrs Fabre. Indeed I would.'

She rang the bell. Rebecca, who must have been waiting from habit in the wings, arrived with the champagne in its silver bucket.

'Essington, did that nice-looking man next door really steal the monotypes?'

'No, Aunt, it was the valuer.'

'Ah, I'm so glad to hear that. You don't like to feel you're losing your judgement.'

'You, Aunt? That's not possible. It was your judgement proved them stolen in the first place.'

'You didn't believe me, did you?'

'I was somewhere in the middle. I really didn't know at all.'

'Ah! Just like your father. But you rushed in somehow and came out with the ball.'

'Something like that.'

Dinner was a roast topside of beef with three vegetables: carrots, potatoes and onions. I could see across the table that the nurse was greatly relieved.

After breakfast I left it up to Hampton to decide what to do with her charge. It would take a few days for her to work out the rules of the game.

I peered from between my shutters at Clyde pacing about with his dogs, no doubt doing the worst thing in the world—waiting for a phone call. It could be that theology developed out of the anguish of waiting for messages—smoke signals, carrier pigeons, letters, phone calls and now the telex. I was buggered if I was going to use the telex.

I sat down and wrote another missive to Feathers. More or less a summary of events to date. Then, because it helped me to understand what had happened, I compiled a little sequence of cause and effect, written as a list for the Holt mind to study in detail. Things seemed to fit together pretty conclusively even though there were questions unanswered and faces missing. And one role was played out of character.

Why had Clyde Warner agreed with the Steves' claim that he

employed them? He had never disclaimed responsibility for their presence. It wasn't in his nature to use thugs. He could look after himself. He had remained calm even with me waving the gun around. He had responded immediately to Jean-Pierre's call. He wouldn't hide behind hired muscle . . . or would he?

He had been trying to obscure something: the fact that things went further? Had he figured that once mad I couldn't be stopped? It remained a question.

I walked around to the Plage de Passable and swam across to Villefranche where, in Aunt's opinion, the loose women were. They certainly weren't on the beach. But then maybe they didn't court tans. In their stead were children.

At school we used to learn, it was in our book, '*Jeudi est le jour de vacances/Toutes les enfants restent en lit*,' or something like that. But now they had Wednesdays off instead. Their presence transformed the beach, gave it life, a sense of future.

What had been the rock star's villa was still shuttered. There was no boat lying on the concrete swimming platform. It seemed curiously desolate, the ensemble—palm trees, the lot.

I made a note to add the Chicago art collector to my list of outstanding problems. Looking at the house I found myself unable to believe in him either.

I swam to the steps. The waters of the Mediterranean are certainly clear, particularly in the harbour at Villefranche. From the surface I could see the outboard motor, memento of that night of my insanity, so distant now that Aunt sat in her house slowly dying. Yet it was my terrible potential and maybe an aspect of my father that linked me to her. Was I her brother's spirit projected forward through time?

I lay a long while on the sand soaking in the sun.

In the afternoon I returned to the drawings. I abandoned the Degas imitations—surely there were enough reproductions of the six already—and worked instead on what I suppose is the definitive Côte d'Azur picture: a window, shutters, interior and the shining land and sea outside.

Late in the afternoon I went to the kitchen to attempt conversation with Rebecca. We had managed to communicate when I had been searching for the oven and the mangle, and now I was hoping that she would prove patient enough to do a little language tutoring on the side. She seemed to enjoy it, laughed a lot and we got far enough for me to suggest that we try it regularly for whatever indeterminate period of time I would be around.

I had established a routine that would make a perfectly acceptable life over the coming weeks. Maybe months, or years. Aunt looked well enough for it to be years.

At dinner, as though reading my thoughts, Aunt observed, 'You need some French, Essington. You can't hang about here stuck among the English. If you want English people they are much nicer over there in England, believe me. There's a language course, you know, just over the bay. It's quite well thought of. You could try that.'

'I don't think I'm the student type, Aunt. And I'm not sure how long I can hang about being supported either.'

'What? You don't want to watch the death scene? I suppose it's gone out of fashion.'

'Not that at all. I wouldn't . . .'

'Then stay, and don't be a fool. I like to have my own flesh and blood about the place. You realize these things too late. The course though—why not give it a try?'

'Actually, I started a little conversation today, with Rebecca. She doesn't seem to mind.'

'Why should she, for heaven's sake. I pay her.'

Hampton was a great hand at the boozing. We came close to knocking off a bottle a head, St Emilion, 1969. Quite a drop. It was English movie night on TV Monte Carlo: *High Society*.

Chapter 17

'Dr Winter. I believe you've met my nephew, Essington Holt.'

We were on the terrace. In the distance, behind Sophie's fixed smile, I could see Clyde Warner. Had he had his phone call yet? The dogs were on the prowl.

Winter and I shook hands. 'Ah, yes, Holt. Heard from our mutual friend?'

'Nice to see you again, doctor.'

'And Essington,' Aunt pressed on with pretended innocence, 'You know Mlle Vaujour?'

'Yes, Aunt, we've met. How are you, Sophie?'

She held out her hand for me to shake.

Did it ever rain that side of the Rhône? We stood awkwardly, bathed in sunshine. Stood in silence.

Renardo wheeled out the drinks trolley. Nurse Hampton rubbed her hands.

'So sorry. And this is Nurse Hampton, come to look after me for a little while. Dr Winter, Mlle Vaujour.'

Everybody was suddenly charmed; charmed, it seemed from their expressions, to a degree previously considered impossible.

Renardo was done up in a white jacket and black tie. He had a slightly stooped carriage and a demeanour expressive of nothing less than absolute loss. He was perfectly cast as a waiter.

Winter was not as jumpy as last time but he still looked like a man who preferred to be between places than at them. 'You are unwell, Mrs Fabre?' He cleaned his glasses on the back of a silk tie.

'Marginally, Dr Winter. Health comes and goes. Nothing to concern ourselves about. Please think of Nurse Hampton as an old woman's self-indulgence.'

'We must all take care of ourselves.' Dr Winter patted the top of his springy hair with the flat of his hand. I wondered, looking at him, if he had a change of clothes. Or maybe he bought everything by the dozen.

Like a country dance, Sophie, Aunt and Hampton became locked in conversation leaving the men free to talk of what?

Winter led me to the drinks trolley and the unmoving figure of Renardo. He tried to pour himself another Perrier water but was beaten to the draw.

'Monsieur?' Renardo asked me.

'No thanks . . . *pas maintenant, merci*.' I was content to hold my Pernod glass, rattling the ice-cubes. If I was to regain lost ground with Sophie I'd need all of what wits I had.

'Tell me, Essington, did you manage with the old lady about the Degas?'

'Perfectly, doctor.'

'Col, it's Col.'

I smiled. 'She didn't tell you, Col?'

He shook his head but seemed content.

We stood. I rattled the ice-cubes some more.

'All's well that ends well,' he proclaimed.

'What's that again?'

'It's Shakespeare.'

He brought out a neat little gold cigarette-case. Offered it to me.

'No thanks. Reformed.'

'Half your strength.' Renardo snapped a gold lighter into flame before you could say Napoleon Bonaparte.

Winter walked around in a circle, stopped, inhaled deeply, let the smoke ooze out of nose and mouth. So much of it, as though he was burning inside. Maybe he was.

I smiled at Renardo, hoping to share my sense of comedy. He nodded back gravely.

'I like it out here. Cap Ferrat has real style. Monte Carlo, Monaco; it's all right, Essington, but all built up. It's a business world. Out here, I like it. It's dripping class. This chap next door. I caught a glimpse of him before, just ambling in his garden. What's his game? What do you reckon?'

'Col,' I caught him by the arm. 'I'm not sure but I think that's Cary Grant. Isn't it?'

'It's not Cary Grant, Essington. Cary Grant is dead.'

He started tapping one foot.

I sipped my drink.

Aunt led Sophie over to us.

'I was just saying to Mlle Vaujour that working for an Australian, she should take advantage of the low dollar and visit our country.'

'What a good idea. I've lots of friends I'm sure would make you very welcome.'

'How nice, Mr Holt.'

Now Aunt led Winter away. Nurse was standing at the trolley, apparently transfixed by the view.

'Sophie, I'm terribly sorry. I got it all wrong.'

'That's perfectly all right. I expect you do it often.'

'Behave like that?'

'No, get everything wrong. It was nice to know you thought I was a thief.'

'I didn't say that. I imagined it was part of your job, that's all. I'm very sorry.'

'Don't worry about a thing.'

More guests arrived. The Nichollses, a very small man with a shining head in company with an equal-sized woman with short clipped blue hair. And Major and Mrs Armitage. Mrs Armitage was quite a bit younger than the Major and knocked back her first whisky like she'd just come in from a fox hunt. All Australians. The Major and Mr Nicholls were terribly pleased to meet a chap recently out from Aussie.

'No nationalism left, that's the problem. You've got to love a country or get out.'

'Certainly, Major. And you live at . . . ?

'Menton, keep a flat in Monte Carlo. Financial interests, that sort of thing.'

'You must get terribly homesick?'

'Well, I do, yes. But with the country falling into the kinds of hands it is . . . all those ethnics. Crikey, what option's a man got?'

Nicholls had restaurants in Sydney. He had to get out too. Maybe because the cash economy was getting dicey. Just before we went into lunch he popped a tablet in his mouth. For the ticker?

Winter and Nicholls and Armitage got on like a house on fire. It

120

wasn't till dessert that Sophie showed the slightest sign of forgiveness. Through most of the meal she feigned interest in Armitage's tirades against tax and subsidies and your Frogs and Eyeties who weren't any good at fighting. It was the Frogs' cowardice in the field that finally forced her to turn my way. I gained points by asking, a fraction loud, if he'd served in Europe or the Pacific.

'Why,' Aunt broke in, 'the Major wouldn't be old enough.'

She was on Armitage's other side and proceeded to describe the circumstances under which her brother got himself killed—charging in anger an unassailable machine-gun post on Crete.

'Sophie, I can't keep on saying I'm sorry.'

But she was too engaged listening to Aunt's tale.

'Is it a family madness?' Sophie asked me.

'That? I've heard that story so many times.'

Nurse Hampton was explaining a death to Mrs Armitage. 'He got to be so light you could have lifted him with one finger. It was right through him, you see; riddled with it.'

'Renardo.' Aunt pointed to Hampton's glass and the macabre conversational flow was stemmed.

After the guests were gone and Nurse was banished to her room to recover her wits, Aunt called for me to join her in a post-mortem. 'Well, Essington, how do you think we Australians go as expatriates?'

'Ghastly, Aunt. If you don't mind my saying so.'

'Well, let that be a warning. That's what you're stuck with down here. They've been here years already, can't make themselves understood or understand what's being said. The world is the *Herald Tribune* and those English snippets on Monte Carlo radio.

'I think it's a different story with the girl. She has a French world to disappear into when she can't take us any more. I must write and apologize for the seating. Now I think you'd better trot along.'

It was uncharacteristic of Aunt to tire so quickly. Or was I interpreting effects now I knew the cause.

Half-way through the following week Aunt was carted off to hospital in Monaco with a thrombosis in her leg. She required anti-coagulants and a couple of days' observation.

Nurse Hampton took the opportunity for a trip into Italy, to San Remo. I found the quiet of the house overpowering despite afternoon conversations with Rebecca during which I felt I made a little progress—I also had a book and a course of tapes to try to build my vocabulary.

I felt that the house was Aunt, that she and its stones were one and the same thing. Even the paintings lost meaning without her. I had the nasty feeling she was not going to come back.

As a distraction I rang Clyde and arranged to drop over, waited for the withdrawal of the dogs, then proceeded.

The same man–boy, immaculate, in control. He was keeping himself clean with an almost spotless apron, white over habitual white. The apron had three or four elegantly placed blobs of colour. There had been boys like Clyde at school: always clean no matter what games they played.

'So you've joined the working class?'

A grin. 'I guess you could say that, Essington. Caught in my own trap. Remember, it's your trade as well.'

'Hey, wait a minute. Once! I've tried once.'

'And the dogs hanging on my wall?'

'That could be or it couldn't. Depends on your point of view.'

We were walking downstairs to a basement area. Clyde opened the door and there it was, the forger's studio. A large space lit by windows along the front wall and by dropped fluorescent tubes. Laid out a bit like an architect's office: several drawing-boards, drying racks, photographic equipment, easel, trolleys with paint palettes.

'They certainly rang,' I said.

'Yep, they rang all right.'

'Who?'

'That's the worst part. I just don't know.'

'If you'd given me a bit of time with that yellow-haired thug we might have found out more: more names, more details.'

'You should watch that,' Clyde warned.

'Watch what?'

'That streak. Nothing's worth it. You become a creature of the same kind. That's loss, not victory.'

'It must worry you though. What happens when you've done

what they want? They'll send another lot after you. You must realize you're dispensable in the end.'

'Essington, I'll work that out when it happens.'

'That's why you pretended you were responsible for the Steves?'

'That's right, an election for the simple life. And to satisfy that moral rectitude of yours.' He held up a Cézanne water-colour: a couple of the pines of Provence, a rock face, ochres, greens, umber, a lot of white paper, pencil marks. 'You like it?'

'They wanted that?'

'*Carte blanche.* As long as they're believable. What are believable have to be minor works; little lost wonders.'

'Your Chicago art dealer?' I asked.

'Who?'

'The man who wanted his villa minded.'

He was stumped for a second. 'Oh, him . . . a figment of the forger's imagination.'

'But why, Clyde?'

'Before I tell you, Essington, remember I'm your only collector. I bought those dogs because I liked them. And because I knew they'd been done from next door. I thought I knew why you'd done them, and the Degas for that matter. And I did nothing. Claiming those guys was just a way of calling you off. You thought I'd set them on to you. My invisible bosses thought you worked for me. Me, I wanted peace. Have for years. I got all the violence I could take when they put us ashore . . . we were kids, understand? Full of moral rectitude like you. Tell me, Essington, how'd you get to stay so morally upright?'

'Me?'

'Yes, you . . . charging around life carrying out your little judgements.'

'So, who owns the villa?'

'This might sound like a tall tale but I believe it's one of your lot. One of your nationalistic businessmen who pulled out when he saw commodity markets start to go.'

He was showing me a lightly sketched study of a scrawny girl standing nude, weight more on one leg than the other. Very geometrically constructed but still naturalistic. Pinned all around her were reproductions of the other studies and drawings for

123

Seurat's *Models in the Studio*. 'A bit chancy, this one. He did so few things. But I think it's a possibility.'

'Do they look at them?'

'Would that it was so easy, but no. They're after a job lot, about twenty pieces in all. Think of it as a disease of the modern world, Essington . . . even forgery is debased. They leave it to me to make them plausible. They're not interested—wouldn't know anyhow. Heaven help me if they can be picked as fakes. I'm to live forever on the line.'

'So who bought the Degas?'

'They bought them.'

'And the Marquet?'

'The same.'

'They paid nothing like Jean-Pierre's price?'

'Nothing like it.'

'And you trust him?'

'What's the point, Essington? Why not trust him? What do you live by in Australia? Some kind of tribal law? It all comes and goes. Jesus, why am I alive? You can't even begin to imagine how many of us aren't. Or they don't have faces any more or lie in beds somewhere in the Midwest. Do you realize there are still hospitals filled with the remains of those kids who were pushed by mad generals? Leave it alone, Essington. Believe me, nothing's worth your soul.'

'But you must have some idea who these people are.'

'Whatever idea I have I wouldn't tell you. That's a promise. Anyway, you've got the information we extracted from that sad young man at Jean-Pierre's gallery . . . Didn't you follow that up?'

'Sort of yes and no. Now I've got other problems, domestic problems. My aunt's very ill.'

'Sorry to hear it.' He looked as if he meant it. All heart, Clyde. Heart and business.

'But you could do something for me,' he said, after a pause.

'Yes?'

'You could sell me the Degas horses.'

'Why should I do that?'

'It's one more I don't have to do.'

We were looking at a set of photos of paintings: highly coloured interiors, unambitious pictures made in the 1930s.

'Going for a bit of Matisse?'

'They want Impressionists; that's what they say, but Matisse is so easy. Particularly materials and ageing.'

'They want Impressionists?'

'Don't start thinking, Essington. Please don't start thinking.'

'Have you ever met this man Winter?'

'Yes, I have. I went to school with him. He's got a cattle ranch in New Mexico.' He laughed. 'I've never met anyone you want to meet, Essington.'

I loved the work Clyde was doing. Just as I had loved my own attempts. I adored the smells, the textured paper, the sense of the artist's craft. Maybe forgery was the way for art to survive the heavy hands of theorists. 'I'll give you the horses as tuition fees. If I wouldn't be in the way.'

He shook my hand. 'And no violence, Essington. Whatever happens in the business happens.'

'You've got the dogs. It's not as if you leave it all to God. You protect yourself.'

'OK, Essington. I protect myself. But that's all.'

Along one wall Clyde had pinned up the returned Degas brothel pictures, all in a row, like the pretty maids in a nursery rhyme.

'A kind of valueless bonus,' he commented. 'Yet a lot of work went into those. You wouldn't believe it.'

'Yes, I would.'

Clyde Warner was in control of himself, confident. Maybe he already had a way out. He'd seen a lot of life.

Chapter 18

Old people develop a defence mechanism. Not so much against death as against the dread and maybe even more, the indignity of it. So Aunt was in a pretty sprightly mood when I arrived at the hospital.

'How was it last night, Aunt?'

'Same as a hotel only more protective. It's good to get away from that house at last.'

'And they look after you well?'

'Like a queen. You must remember this is not one of your jumped-up republics. There are still values in Monaco, though God knows what they are. They know me here. I've been in before. This is not my first time. Nor, I venture to say, will it be my last. Did Renardo bring you?'

'Yes, I asked if he would.'

'You wouldn't nick out and fetch him, would you? I'd just love to see how depressed he can look. Perhaps me laid low will bring a smile.'

He understood what I said and followed me in from where he had been polishing the Bentley. Beside the bed, maybe by association, I thought he looked like a handsome Boris Karloff. He stood, hands clasped in front, holding the chauffeur's hat he never wore but always kept on the seat at his side.

There was a quick interchange in French and then, lo and behold, she got her smile, if a brief one. They shook hands and he departed.

'I can't tell you how fond I am of Renardo.'

The leg was doing fine. She would be back in a couple of days. I told her I'd agreed to the nurse taking a short holiday along the coast and she smiled in a contented sort of way.

Just before I left she said, 'You mustn't give up on things, Essington. Do give that nice girl a ring, won't you?' Contrary advice to Clyde's. He was frightened of my obsessions. At my age I should have been past advice. Was I a kind of child–man?

126

I tried to see Dr Morlino on the way back from the Centre Hospitalier Princess Grace but he was out for the day. It was just for form really. I could ring him later and have my attempts at French misunderstood.

We looped down through Monte Carlo because I felt like it and I peered out of the car windows at every girl we passed in the hope of catching a glimpse of Sophie. Pathetic but true. Then we shot back along the Moyenne Corniche. Renardo loved to give the car a bit of speed: one hundred miles an hour we touched on the antique speedo.

When I rang Sophie was busy till we ran out of days. Polite but busy. Goodbye love.

I got Rebecca to ring the doctor. It was true. Aunt would be back in one more day.

Then I popped over to work with Clyde.

Rodin produced copious numbers of drawings of models in action: jumping, rolling, dancing, standing; naked or in loose flowing drapes. Many of them have a pale wash of one or two colours over the top.

Clyde Warner had decided on a small portfolio of these. He had already procured the paper, not so difficult in France where old methods battle with technology. The bookish arts still thrive.

So paper was not really a problem, as my teacher was at pains to point out; there are still packets of nineteenth-century paper lying in dusty corners all over France. For the Rodins the main concern was to get the quality of line. The original drawings were made very quickly; just capturing the body in the flow of rapid movement. Movement—towards the end of the century they had gone bananas about movement.

It seemed an impossible task to fake these things. The pencil marks made by whoever did the drawings had to be at a speed similar to that of the master, to have the fluidity, to leave the right quantity of graphite on the surface of the paper.

'It's not possible,' I said.

'Well, it's harder, admittedly, because of the situation. They know they're buying fakes, so instead of believing in the product they don't believe in it. That's a problem. You've lost half the game to start with. That is half the regular game.

'In this new game maybe you win something to make up. To pull off a forgery sale you've got to keep the experts out. If that's possible. You've got to get the sale finished so, even if the buyer develops doubts, the last thing he wants is to have those doubts proved. Who wants to be a sucker, Essington?

'Whoever wants these things wants them believable, but isn't going to know more than we do. Chances are they'll know a good deal less. You even get that in public galleries where people win jobs for favours. What's the odds for a group of stand-over men knowing an authentic Rodin line? How many people in the world would know? All we need is a line and a signature.

'A good arrogant line . . . in character with the old megalomaniac. The buyer isn't going to believe in it whatever line it is. But he's got to believe that anybody else will believe. Just because I did it. They've caught me. For them I'm Rodin, or Cézanne or Seurat . . . whoever.'

'Someone told them you were the genius. You know it has to be Jean-Pierre; so do I.'

'No judgements, remember, Essington. We're after a bit of grace while the sun sinks. You more or less promised, no judgements.'

'Why the hell don't you force it out of him?'

'If I know it already there's nothing to force out.'

I had to swallow hard to accept this lie-down-and-take-it attitude; I swallowed hard. Then spent the afternoon flipping up slides of Rodin drawings and running lines quickly over sheet after sheet of paper. These were going to be Rodins produced on a percentage system . . . not unlike the monkey and the typewriter: if you had enough of each and enough time you'd get a Shakespeare sonnet.

That was assuming the monkey didn't think.

Aunt came home and, that evening, Nurse, complete with a terrible little hat with a peak and San Remo written all over it.

'You know, I rather like her, Essington.' Hampton had gone up to her room to change into uniform. 'Underneath that starched exterior she's really just a drunken old tart. Quite a find, wouldn't you say?'

'Your leg, Aunt, how is it?'

'I think we've got it under control. Dr Morlino says a couple of whiskies might be good, in the evening. Does something for the blood but I can't for the life of me remember what.'

'It puts alcohol into it.'

'That's what it does. They were all quite sweet over there. It's very clean . . . rather American. It's an American Royal family after all. Like that . . . what's her name?'

I couldn't think of anybody.

'Simpson. Like that Mrs Simpson.'

On a visit to Nice, I found a bookshop near the old Ecole de Beaux Arts where I purchased a book devoted entirely to abstract art—starting with Kandinsky and moving through to Rothko and Frank Stella. I put a card inside it and posted it to Sophie—a lovelorn gesture.

Dull depressing days passed with Aunt slipping away. Yet always the little ball of a chin stuck out and a smile pulled her lips back from her teeth.

The high spots were working with Clyde and collecting snippets from his store of knowledge of nineteenth- and twentieth-century art.

Once I asked: 'Have you tried abstracts? Mondrian for instance? They'd be money for jam.'

'Curiously, they aren't.' His Seurat was accumulating age by degrees. It was a striking painting, no more than forty centimetres in the biggest dimension. Clyde had kept the pointillist colour application broad, as Seurat did in his studies.

'In abstracts,' he explained, 'you don't have subject to command the viewer's attention and your market is very much more limited. If you miss with a Mondrian even a dog can see straight off it's no good . . . there's nothing else there to look at. And, technically, his paint cracked. It was in long unbroken surfaces, nowhere for it to expand and contract. Contracting, Essington, is what paint spends most of its time doing. The canvas does both, depending on atmosphere. It's hard to get it to crack right. I go for blobby pictures with as little overpainting as possible—no glazing. There's less fiddling about.'

'I thought it would be easier.'

'Your great abstracts, very hard to simulate. Harder still to off-load. The great democratic art form is imitation of nature, one kind or another. That's what people want when they make their pile. A portrait of Mr and Mrs and lots of pictures of things.'

After a couple of months, during which Nurse took over the management of life bit by bit and Aunt spent more time bombed out on pain-killers, I was summoned to the half-lit room, sat down and instructed.

I was to go to London. Apply for a visa. 'You are close, I believe, to outstaying the welcome of the French Government, Essington. In these times of bombings I'm not sure that is wise. They are very relaxed people, the French, but when they want to get nasty they can get as nasty as anyone. Believe me.'

So, that was arranged for a week hence.

The book, all three francs eighty worth of it, elicited a bland thank-you card. After that, nothing. The idea of the trip to England appealed because travel was an excuse for writing letters to the unbending Mlle Vaujour.

The day before I was to fly out of Nice I went to eat at the Nichollses. It was a return invitation. I was representing Aunt.

It was during that week that Clyde lost his Indo-Chinese help: result of tightened immigration controls. She had crossed over the border.

Which border?

He thought probably into Germany.

'Those bombers. They are supposed to be supporting the downtrodden. The group who really suffer from their terrorism consists of those who can't defend themselves: the international refugees.'

'Is it easy to find a replacement?'

'Massive unemployment. Particularly over this side. But I'm not sure I want anyone. With her it was all right. Get a card-carrying Frenchman and he's going to start wondering why I work in so many styles. They might suspect me of something.'

Nicholls had bought himself a ritzy pad right near the Monte Carlo Country Club with a view of under- and overpasses corkscrewing into the sacred Grimaldi stamping ground. As a background to the concrete, they had the sea.

They were very pleased with themselves, the Nichollses. They didn't just have the apartment. Not at all. Nothing cheap about the little pair.

'She's my dream, I love her.' He shook his cocktail shaker.

'Fifteen metres, that's a nice size.'

'Well, she does us. It was a bit of luck really.' He puffed out his chest. 'Luck, and an eye for a deal. Of course, you've got to have the cash, Holt.'

He'd actually shaken up a stunner of a cocktail—the sort of thing you might use to tranquillize a Brahman bull.

'Fellow over from Guernsey, got into some kind of financial mess, had to sell up quick smart. A gift!'

'You never take it out, Alf.'

'Sarah's not a seagoing woman.'

'And neither are you a seagoing man.' She held my forearm. 'Only he won't admit it.'

Mrs Nicholls was resplendent in a gold-lamé jump suit and matching earrings—loops big enough for a circus rabbit to leap through.

But I didn't mind her. She gave the impression of seeing the joke.

'He called it *Sydney Dreaming*,' she laughed; a wonderful wheezy cough–laugh.

'Of course, Holt, it's just a tender beside our Prince's craft.'

It was nice to think of the two of them perched up there looking out over water through which once the long trading boats of the Phoenicians sailed.

Major Armitage and his wife arrived. Was she pleased to see Essington . . . It was embarrassing.

We all got into discussing who was the most likely Aussie Mogul to take over which company and who looked good in the football.

In came Dr Winter. My heart leapt at the sight of him then sank on finding him alone. His guppy eyes ogled the world through the miracle of modern optics.

'Essington!' Almost as though we had been at dancing class together.

'Nice to see you, Winter.'

They collectively smiled with pleasure at having ensnared a recruit—me. Mrs Armitage smiled more than anybody else. She was pointing out to me a clump of apartments down towards the Casino where she and the Major rested their heads when not in Menton. Mrs Nicholls was out in the kitchen rattling things about. I had believed that once you'd cheated the world and retired with your stash you gave up cooking and sent out for reheated salmonella. I had believed wrong.

I heard Winter telling Nicholls and the Major that there were still tax loopholes in Australia. 'There's art, John.' (John must have been the Major's name.)

And when I looked around the good doctor was looking straight at me. Assuming he could see that far.

'Art, Col? What do you mean there's art?' Alf Nicholls pushed home for the information.

'Not now. This is relaxation. Drop by some time at the office and we'll talk.' He walked over to where I was being breathed upon by the Major's wife. 'How's your aunt, Essington?'

'She wished she could have been here today. But, to tell you the truth, she's going to be crook for a couple of months yet.'

'But it's not . . . nothing serious, is it?' They all knew what that meant.

'Jesus Christ, no. Fit as a Mallee bull.'

Chapter 19

Winter and I were again face to face over seafood cocktails.

'You've an interest in art yourself, haven't you, Essington? Sophie showed me the book you sent her.'

'Only a small interest. Just abstract art.'

'Oh, do you, Mr Holt,' screamed Mrs Armitage. 'That's my favourite too.'

'Yeah, I like Frank Stella best,' I said. 'He's so spiritual.'

'Oh, yes.' She clapped her hands. 'Ethereal.'

'And you, Dr Winter, what do you like?'

'I'm involved in business, Essington. I don't find the time to be a connoisseur.'

'That's a pity; I'm sure you'd like Frank Stella. He does big circles—concentric. They're electrifying.' Would he catch the sarcasm?

'I'm sure they are.'

'And what sort of art did I hear you recommending before, Dr Winter?'

'Not so much the art. The tax arrangements.' The magic words 'tax arrangements' arrested all attention; except for Mrs Nicholls who retreated to the kitchen, carting away the empty stemmed glasses that had held the seafood cocktails.

Mrs Armitage lost interest in Stella's transcendental qualities and directed her thoughts to the general outline of tax advantages available to those who buy art.

'Mind you, there's still film investment but that's not as attractive as it was. And there're the incentives relating to high technology projects receiving Australian Government approval—projects which become eligible for the scheme.'

The good Dr Winter adored his counselling role—the born economic–legal psychologist. As he revealed this side of himself to the shells of people hanging on his words, it seemed to me that there was a childishness about them all. I was tempted to remove Winter from my list of suspects—despite the garbled testimony of Yellow-Hair. I felt sure I was peering at one of the new people—innocents who simply believed in what the world was becoming.

'Firstly, you're looking at the possibility of depreciation. I don't want you to think of art *per se*, but rather art as furniture. Your art becomes your furniture. But unlike a steel filing cabinet or a computer, the painting on your office wall increases in value while it is getting its purchase price written off as depreciation. Get it?'

Sarah Nicholls wheeled in a warming trolley with the next course: pork chops cooked with canned pineapple rings.

Investment advice gave way to food distribution and discussion of the Bordeaux wine. But you could see that Winter, mind jogging on the spot to keep warm, was ready to take off again on art investment as soon as opportunity presented.

'Then, and these things are not mutually exclusive, you have the possibility of gifting art works direct to a public gallery. In this case you deduct the value of the work from taxable income.'

'Don't see much in that one,' said the Major. 'You get off what you pay out. Might as well increase expenses.'

'That depends on your valuation,' said Winter with a smug grin.

'You mean the value isn't linked to market price?' asked Alf Nicholls, semi-catching on.

'It can be challenged. The tax people can demand that it be demonstrated in the market.'

'But you could already have done that,' Nicholls thought aloud. 'You could put it through auction. It'd only cost the commission. Maybe you could do a deal on that anyway.'

'So,' advised the doctor, nodding approval, 'you make your own market.'

Sarah Nicholls was contentedly munching on the fat of her pork chop, while staring blankly along the table at her husand. 'It sounds like open slather to me,' she said. 'You make your own market because the work's got no value on any kind of external scale. And your value is accepted as the going price.'

'Just like I said,' Mrs Armitage smiled at me. 'Frank what-was-his-name-again? He's terrific!'

'Stella,' I prompted.

'God! I love that man's art,' she smiled. 'Extra-sensory!'

'To sum up.' Nicholls puffed himself up as though he was in a boardroom. The pink face beneath the gleaming head turned bright red. 'You get your art. You write it off. You push the market at the same time and then you off-load on to the public galleries. It's neat, but the galleries couldn't hold the pictures. All the world and his dog would be into that one.'

'That is the hitch,' Winter agreed. 'But I do believe there's an answer.'

I had been a good boy and devoured my meat and fruit and veg. The rest now set to catching up. A calm had entered the room, the calm of contentment. Brains were doing additions and subtractions. Maybe they could beat those bastards out to get their money after all. They could beat them one more time.

'I don't think anyone's tasted anything I've cooked for years,' said our hostess. 'That's the problem being married to a restaurant-owner. Oh, we chew away all right . . . then we count the money.'

'Can't afford to let things slip,' the Major advised. 'That was beautiful, Sarah.' A prompted afterthought.

Dessert wine with ice-cream and fruit salad. Had they turned childish dreams into late-life reality? Through hoarding and tax evasion—a kind of financial magic.

I managed to leave by teaming up with the restless Dr Winter. He was sober as an accountant, taking care of business with his Perrier water.

On our way out of the security building he said how sorry he was that we didn't see more of each other. With Gerald Sparrow in common we really should get together. Then he patted his hair. 'It's time, Essington. There just isn't enough of it in the day.'

'Not a problem for me, I assure you. One of the great unemployed.'

'Well, with you it's different. You're on a kind of holiday, I expect.'

'Mixed. Mainly holiday. Tell me, do you have a lot of clients like the Nichollses and the Armitages? There's quite an Australian community here, isn't there?'

'It grows, particularly now that money flows so much faster

around the world. People feel less locked into their own systems.'

'Do many get involved in this art collecting?'

'Professional secrets, Essington.' He held a finger to his lips and blinked.

'I was only thinking of Aunt and the insurance problems.'

'Of course you were, Essington.'

I wondered if Sophie had passed my suspicions on to him.

'Of course you were. And quite rightly too. As you can imagine though . . . these old people, alone . . . they've got too much time to think. Not enough to do.'

'Yes, but what if I told you that Aunt had been right all along. The pictures were faked and changed over. What would you say about old ladies then?'

'Hypothetical, Essington.'

We were outside standing mid flowering plants in raised concrete troughs painted pink ochre—the Monaco national colour. Mostly oleanders, deadly poisonous but pretty in their pinks and whites.

'Not hypothetical, Dr Winter. That's fact and it doesn't stop there.'

The aquarium face that I had learnt to trust over lunch turned just a little hard. The lips pressed together and eyebrows lowered behind the glasses. He did not pat his head.

'Please pass on my warm regards to Mlle Vaujour,' I begged. We shook hands and I wandered off through an anti-pedestrian world to find a bus—the Menton–Nice line.

On the way home I wondered who would advise people like the Nichollses on their paintings. To date they had collected framed photos of grinning children, perhaps their own. One, a daughter, had bands on her teeth. No doubt they were all grown up now.

Perhaps Mrs Armitage had a few transcendental works. I had the idea that she had said 'Stella' the way a parrot might; a slow witted parrot.

That night I sent a card to Feathers telling him to reply to another letter I had sent, it seemed, quite some time ago.

Chapter 20

Ten o'clock the following morning I was in London. You could live in Nice and work a couple of days a week on the Thames. Oh, what an un-Australian sensation.

I went straight to the Consulate to apply for a visa for France, filled in forms, then headed off to Old Bond Street. I was keen to get back to Aunt.

Grantley Simpson was expecting me. I had rung a couple of days before. He worked in a nasty little upstairs room from which, through the windows, he could see a brick wall ornamented with sewerage pipe painted cream, then rusted.

He wore a grey cardigan pulled out of shape by weights in its pockets. When I left I had the impression of slippers. But he wouldn't have been wearing those, would he? He had a white transparent skin with little rivers of blood crowding together to create the illusion of pink cheeks.

His gloomy room was all paper and books.

'What a pleasure. Ah, yes, your aunt. And those Degas. Wouldn't it have been nice had they been real.'

'Very nice indeed, Mr Simpson.'

'Yes, very nice, very nice. Would you like a cup of tea?'

'Only if you were about to . . .'

'I'm always about to have a cup of tea. A nice hot cup of tea. You can't beat it.'

He rammed the cord into the jug. There was a pop.

'Oh! Blast! Always doing that.'

Blown element. Not to be defeated out came a pair of pliers, instantly located on one of a wall of shelves, and he set to remedying the fault.

'It's a throwaway society, Mr Holt. But I'm not part of it.' He chuckled. 'Through scholarship I inhabit another era. Degas and I walk the world together. Only I'd like to think

137

that I'm a little easier to get along with.'

He held his trophy high to view against the light. The burnt-out wire hung loose where it had parted. While he was winding the ends about each other conversation continued.

'Have you heard of Madame Foissy who owned a house in the Rue Payenne, Paris?'

'Rue Payenne,' he corrected my pronunciation. 'Indeed I have.'

'She had a son.'

'I know, I know. Unfortunately he died; oh, it must have been 1958 or thereabouts. 1958 I believe it was.'

'Would you believe me, Mr Simpson, if I told you that my aunt bought her Degas from old Mr Foissy a few years before he died. In a box full of photos?'

'I would believe you, indeed I would; only your aunt's Degas were not Degas. She led me to believe that she knew that.'

'But did she tell you the story of Mr Foissy?'

'No tale can make a picture become what it is not.'

'I read your report, Mr Simpson.'

'There, it's in. Now for our tea.'

'I read the report and you didn't give the impression of having looked at the pictures at all.'

But he had gone out the door for water.

He was replying as he came back down the corridor. 'What I said, if I remember, was that they did not exist . . . there was no reference to them. Had they been real, then they would have existed.'

Now he listened for the first rumblings of the heating process. 'Ah, there she blows.'

'Then there's no room for a new Degas?'

'For a real one, yes, of course. A real one would be part of what exists. How, I wonder, would your aunt have made contact with old Mr Foissy? He died, unfortunately, before I heard of his existence.'

I repeated the story as Aunt had told it. He very nearly had a seizure when I came to the bit about the photos.

'Degas photos destroyed?'

'I'm afraid that's the story, Mr Simpson. But it's no loss, really. If Aunt's monotypes weren't the real thing the photos wouldn't be either.'

The jug was spilling water all around itself, into an intermediate zone where a wooden bench top gave way, by degrees, to piles of paper. At that point the paper was discoloured and growing mould.

It was tea-bags, just hot water and tea-bags.

'Round about the time of Mrs Fabre's visit, Mr Holt, another Degas was brought in for me to see. Just one, identical to one of your aunt's. Funny thing, first we get unknown monotypes and then they are all over the place.'

'Someone brought one in to you? What sort of someone, Mr Simpson? Would you remember?'

'Of course I would. I remember very clearly. There were two of them. One, a smallish chap with very thick glasses. I couldn't help wondering what he could see of the picture anyway. Of course, I know that sounds cruel. None of us are perfect, Mr Holt.'

'Me, I'm close, Mr Simpson,' I laughed.

'I expect I took a dislike to the two of them, though it was really the other who was unpleasant. They weren't interested in what I thought about their picture. I didn't say much anyway. What they wanted to know was if I'd seen any like it before.

'I'm a cautious man by nature. But I've nothing to hide. I didn't take to this one, like I said. I could sense him laughing at me behind his hand. Arrogant he was, with thin blond hair receding and going a little grey at the edges. I can't put my finger on what it was exactly but they put the wind up me a little. I expect it was because of the picture. They didn't even ask if I thought it was genuine.'

'And you told them about Aunt's pictures?'

'No. That's the point. The cautious side of my nature got the better of me. "Very nice little picture," I said. "Very rare." "Valuable?" they asked. That's all most of them care about now. It's the money, not the art. "Oh, very valuable," I assured them. But even that didn't really seem to be what they wanted to find out.'

We had finished our tea. And now he was filling a pipe. Fixed habits.

I explained to him as best I could about getting Aunt's pictures

139

back and he got terribly excited. 'I would love to see them. Those images were very authentic and now you tell me about Mrs Fabre and Mr Foissy . . . well, it's a very different situation. But, I'll tell you, Mr Holt, you can see the instant you look. If you need more information than that then you don't know your painter. Life's very simple, really.'

'That's what Aunt said. She knew the instant she saw them that they were forged. And her eyesight's about as bad as the man with the glasses. Only she had no glasses to help her out.'

'You know him then? If I remember, they were Australian—I should have said, Australian, or perhaps, Rhodesian.'

'That's gone now.'

'What has?'

'Rhodesia. No, I can't say that I do know him, Mr Simpson. And I wish I could show you the monotypes, but the time's not right. My aunt's a very ill woman. I need to keep things simple—like life.'

'Understood, Mr Holt.'

I promised to keep in touch.

It took two days for the visa to come through. It could have been worse. I spent them in the Tate and the National Galleries looking at pictures from a totally different perspective. The Tate had some avant-garde art, self-conscious works which seemed to me to be about what art was. A kind of investigation.

It struck me that the most advanced artist of them all was the invisible one, Clyde Warner. And it crossed my mind more than once, when looking at pictures that had been donated in recent years, that they could be by Clyde or by the army of his unknown fellow craftsmen.

What they were doing was undermining the pernicious influence of money on art. Real revolutionaries and, like the real frontrunners, unrecognized.

Aunt was a little worse, or so it struck me after the days away. I was pleased to return and be welcomed like a prodigal. As though undergoing a change of personality, she now craved my company.

We abandoned the *Herald Tribune*. 'Too late for that sort of thing, Essington.'

Occasionally she called me Greg—that was my father's name—I

don't think because her faculties were going. It was to meet him through me before death. Was that psychology, Essington?

She liked me to read to her so we embarked on Dickens's *Bleak House*, after an abortive start with Maugham's *Christmas Holiday*, chosen because he had lived on the Cap.

Really, *Bleak House* was a better choice, long as a train but episodic. It sounds a dreadful thing to say but I was learning a lot from Aunt's slow death . . . among other things, that I would die myself and how to do it.

Nurse was a constant presence as was the little row of bottles, each containing tablets or capsules with something very specific in mind.

Feathers' letter arrived coinciding with the entry of the unbending old lawyer in Dickens's plot; walking to his death against the warning of a tolling clock.

'Oh, I love that character,' Aunt exclaimed. 'He's so real.' *Bleak House* was a favourite, read several times before. She didn't like the sentimental passages so much, fidgeted through those.

'Dear Essington,' Feathers wrote. 'Sorry to be so long replying. I didn't know what to say and I don't know what's been happening over there. Whatever the summation of your actions they have not gone unnoticed on this side of the world.

'That is why I did not write, preferring to wait for an outcome. While it is still not clear what has passed between you and, among others, our Dr Winter, it is clear that you have invoked his displeasure and that some at least of his complaints reflect against me, since it was I who suggested that you visit your aunt in the first instance.'

Not true, Feathers. She asked me to come.

'I noted and refuted your earlier comments questioning the veracity of Dr Winter. Now I ask you to refrain from any action which might prejudice him in the conduct of his business. It seems you have done harm and no good . . .'

And so on and so forth.

I sent him a telegram: 'I found the pictures.' And signed it 'Essington'.

There had always been that side to Feathers. But I had never known it to surface as strongly as now.

The letter had little initials and file numbers at the top. It was, I guessed, for general consumption within Richards and Temple. It was clear that whatever Winter had said was designed to put me right out the door.

And Sophie was covering up for him. That's why nothing ever worked with her. Or was she right in on the ground floor? His beautiful partner in crime? Unlikely.

Jean-Pierre might have been a weak bastard; Clyde Warner some kind of Holy Roller forger intent on saving his soul; the thugs, just thugs. But I suddenly realized that there was a whole second story. Finding the Degas had only been a beginning. And I was being locked out by corporate disapproval. Bugger them!

I couldn't do anything but keep on being with Aunt. She, I reasoned, was the higher cause. Sometimes I went next door to join in the fun, but, through repetition, the work there was losing its appeal. Clyde was close to finishing the quota and he was getting tense. What would happen how? More orders? Or would he be in the way?

I hadn't bothered to reply to Feathers' letter; the telegram would suffice. If he chose to go over to the side of a corporation against an old friend—maybe the oldest friend he had—God rot his soul.

Thus I was surprised when he rang.

'Essington, I want to talk to you.'

'There's nothing to talk about.'

'Oh, yes there is.'

'What?'

'You might be right about Winter.'

'I might be right. What's that supposed to mean? Of course I'm right. Feathers, that man's a criminal and you've got him doing Aunt's business. You're out of touch.'

'Be that as it may, Essington. I grant you've got a right to feel like you do. But it's worse than you think. It goes further.'

'Then fix it up.'

'I'm not really in a position to do that.'

'If I was you I'd try.' I hung up.

*

142

Aunt died six weeks later. She was buried up on the hill overlooking Cap Ferrat and the bay. From there she could watch the coming and going of the ships and keep time by the flashing of the lighthouse.

A curt letter from Feathers' secretary knocked me into a heap. I was the main beneficiary of the estate. Me, and in a small way, Renardo and Rebecca who shared the surname Pinci—very French indeed.

I have to admit I expected a legacy. Always had. With Aunt being childless. I'd often fantasized about what I would do with it. My dream? To own my own studio apartment in Chippendale, down from the breweries, just in from Broadway. That had been my dream.

'*Mon rêve,*' as Rebecca would say when attempting to get me to understand that she would like a little house with a patch of ground up in the hills.

It would be a fair time coming, the money, so I could still be me for a while.

Funny, the weather had broken for the funeral. We were a sad group: Hampton, Rebecca, Renardo, me. I took responsibility for not inviting any of the expatriates. High grey cloud obscured the sun and a wind beat in off the sea: a wind born on the dusty coast of Africa.

I rang Winter. Sophie hardly responded when I pronounced my name. Stiff. She put me through. Yes, he had heard of the death. Certainly this was business. If I wanted to take things out of his hands that would be possible. He would wait on an instruction from Richards and Temple. Then that would be that. He was sure all of us in the community would miss Mrs Fabre.

'One more thing, Dr Winter.'

'Mr Holt?' At least he'd dropped the Essington. It had always made me wince, straight from the fish's mouth.

'Why did you bad-mouth me to that firm?'

'To whom?'

'Richards and Temple.'

'I'm sure I don't know what you're talking about.'

'You will.'

'Is that a threat, Mr Holt?'

'That, Winter, is a fact.'

I rang Feathers at home. Got him out of bed at four in the morning and told him what to do. He was not too happy about the intrusion on his sleep.

'Do it by telex, Feathers. Remember telex?'

'I'll do that.'

'How are you all getting along with Winter?'

'Strained, no thanks to you. Nobody will talk to me about it.'

'How do you take Aunt's work away from him then?'

'No problem with that. Simply a direct instruction. Given the situation—may the Lord rest her soul—there won't be any more anyway, will there? He can only do what he has instructions to do.'

'What about renewals . . . things like that, over here?'

'I'll have them transferred.'

'To who?'

'To whom, Essington. Don't attempt to take on the world, will you.'

'We'll see about that. It can get very paranoic making on this side of the world, surrounded by crooks. You need all the friends you can get.'

'Then you need this one as well.'

Maybe he was right . . . maybe not.

There's an Irish song that goes, 'Misfortunes they never come single 'tis plain.' And so it was with the death of Aunt Eloise. It was the start of a bad run.

Chapter 21

My morning swim revealed open shutters all along the ground floor of Villa Florida—Hoodsville. Somebody had taken up residence. For pleasure? Or for something else altogether. Or maybe to combine just a little bit of each. It's so hard to tell these days where one begins and the other ends.

I lounged on the beach; actually pondering what to do with myself. I was stuck in a kind of limbo: inheritor without inheritance and with no clear idea of what it was that had been inherited. Of one thing I was certain. I was a lot richer than I had been and I was going to need a new psychology to go with the money. Living the life of a scunge, dreaming of a break from the anxieties of a hand-to-mouth existence is, I realized, the natural mode of our being. The dream, immense riches, is an abnormality; those who devoted a life to the attainment of the dream were stricken with a kind of madness. What, I wondered, was the condition of those who had riches thrust upon them?

Time would tell me. Till then, stumble along Essington. Worse things could happen to a man.

I swam back to the beach, dressed and returned to the house by the walk around the margin of the sea.

Steps reached the Boulevard Général de Gaulle just around the corner from the Villa du Phare. I was still climbing when I heard a screech of tyres and saw a flash of red. A large familiar American sedan shot off down the road. The grill gate into Warner's house was open. Even from the road you could sense the quiet, the lack of habitation.

At the foot of the steps leading to Warner's terrace a dog lay dead—skull bashed in. A human-sized corpse, one eye staring, amazed, at the unanswering sky. Blood oozing on to terrazzo.

One of the glass doors was smashed, but neatly—the glass broken away leaving a clean wood-framed rectangle to step through. I followed the steps down to where Warner would have been working. The room was vacant; only work materials scattered about. All the forgeries were gone and with them the reference materials. An artist's studio without art. A very empty-looking void.

I started out on the dismal search for a body. I worked my way methodically through the building, room by room; turning handles, throwing open doors, each moment expecting the shock that never came.

In the garden I found the other dog lying where it had dragged itself, semi-conscious, breathing heavily; and in the breath a growl. The glazed eyes watched me, angry perhaps . . . no message passed through the limp torso.

Back inside the house I began a more thorough search: drawers and cupboards, room by room. I got the feeling the job had just been done, with a tooth comb, minutes before. I discovered nothing out of the ordinary, nothing at all.

I rang Aunt's house, Rebecca answered. I managed to ask her to send Renardo over to meet me and to ring for a vet. Country life had conditioned me to a semi-automatic concern for animals; even for those reared to be killed . . . particularly for those.

I rang Jean-Pierre. No answer. With the phone clutched in my hot hand I could picture in my mind, all in a row before me, the open shutters of the Villa Florida . . . its palms, the steps down to the sea.

Renardo was walking up the drive. I'm not sure why I asked him to come. More than anything, I guess, I wanted him to feel what was going on, to sense the reality of the violence. With Aunt gone, Rebecca and Renardo were the closest thing to friends I had in France. Whatever and wherever Clyde was, he was a devious exotic; no fall-back position for my soul.

I led Renardo through the house in one-dimensional French and with each step we took attempted to explain, to give an outline of, the story that grew out of the six monotypes.

He just kept on nodding his long bony head, bloodless lips pressed together.

Hadn't he heard any noise?

No. He had been mowing. The lawn mower, the perfect noise-screen, the petty criminal's friend. But I knew we were out of the league of petty criminals. There was a sure touch in this. It was not the work of Steves or not-Steves, nor of Yellow-Hair. Whoever they were these people were professional, they worked neat.

Was Renardo impressed or not? I couldn't tell. Nothing about him changed. He was silent, helpful, even efficient. He rang through to the police and then we set to work on the wounded dog while it was still shocked and horizontal. I tied a muzzle made of torn sheets into place, bound its great legs, then settled down to await callers.

Again I tried to contact Jean-Pierre. Still no answer. There were a hundred possible reasons for the phone to ring out; none of them felt right.

It was agreed: Renardo would answer questions; I was along because I was there.

The vet, a woman from Nice, didn't want to kill the dog, so, in a moment of weakness, I let her take it away. Renardo gave his uncomplicated statement to the boys from the Prefecture then we were off, headed for the Galerie de la Renaissance in the Citroën brake. On the way I got Renardo to turn down the dead end leading to the gates of Villa Florida. There was a red Buick sitting in the drive and while we turned, I saw a man walk out and lift an armful of paper from the open boot.

We circled back around Cap Ferrat to pick up Rebecca. She protested that she couldn't see a reason to leave the house. Why was she in any kind of danger? Just because people broke in next door!

I had Yellow-Hair's little .22 automatic stuffed in the side pocket of the powder-blue jacket. My heart was pumping Christ-knows-what everywhere through my body.

We dropped Rebecca at the market in the old town behind Nice Port to stock herself up for a change from Australian cuisine. That perked her up a lot.

Heading off for the gallery I plucked up courage to show Renardo the gun. Sad eyes observed it over grey sacks of skin that hung from his lower lids. Again he was not surprised.

'Où se trouve les choses pour tirer cet petit pistolet, Renardo?'
Not a word but we turned west to the rougher end of Nice where

the street girls are. We double-parked outside a small hunting–shooting–fishing shop. He was inside and out again in a second with a box of .22 shorts in his hand. Not much use, a small-bore gun, but better than nothing.

Renardo headed towards the sea then came up the Rue de France until we hit a traffic jam. A sinking feeling in the stomach. I jumped out and ran to where the flashing lights were; the police, the ambulance, the *pompiers*. All outside the Galerie de la Renaissance.

'*Qu'est-ce que c'est le problème?*' I asked an elderly woman standing watching.

'I wish I knew, young man. I just asked the same question myself and couldn't comprehend a word of the reply.'

Back at the car I asked Renardo to walk down and investigate while I took my place standing by the driver's door like all the rest of us who couldn't escape the traffic snarl. The orchestra was tuning up for another horn symphony.

I knew what had happened. My pulse told me and so did the emptiness, the hollowness. Then a terrible nausea filled the vacuum.

No connection seemed to be made between the attack on the house next door—that didn't rate newspaper mention anyway—and the double homosexual suicide on the Rue de France that the next day's *Nice Matin* featured on page three.

Of course the homosexual theory had to help explain Clyde Warner's general reluctance to pass judgement on his friend. Maybe he was now dead because of that reluctance.

The thought had rattled around at the back of my mind that Villa du Phare might be the next target for attack: thus Rebecca's removal. It had the Degas, it had me. When we returned we found it still in one piece.

Rebecca's outing had been justified, if not on account of safety, then by the large baked fish that adorned the table when I sat down in solitary splendour to eat. But I couldn't eat. Alone, confused, I was beginning to regret Nurse's professional and instant departure after the funeral.

By the time I had finished the Sancerre, Domaine du Fort, I was consumed by rage. All I could think of was 'Charge' and yet, for the first time in my life, I sensed a little of Aunt's worldliness. Had I got it as a gift with the money? So I didn't run straight off down the road—thank Christ. Those killers would not respond to a simple bang over the ear. I started plotting a fantasy of action. The same Essington but doing it in his head; in technicolour.

Renardo and Rebecca were absent-mindedly wiping their plates with bread while staring up at the *Dallas* regulars on TV shaping for yet another family brawl.

My sudden recognition of a certain domesticity made me, for an instant, ashamed. I had, till then, granted them a fraction less existence than I allowed myself. They looked around, surprised by the intrusion; embarrassed too.

'I'm sorry,' I explained in French. 'This is not like my life in Australia. Aunt,' I said unnecessarily, 'was a very rich woman.'

That was my excuse for intrusion.

They seemed to accept it in good part. Then, I guess, I told them lots of things they knew—they had eyes. They had seen me go next door day after day. I told them both things I had told Renardo already.

'These problems started with Mrs Fabre, with her pictures. That is why she brought me here.' I don't think that was news either. 'The situation is dangerous. I am a stranger. It is difficult.'

Renardo stood up and walked towards me. Without changing expression he took my hand and shook it. It seemed a very serious gesture.

Then he smiled like he had at Aunt's bedside at Monaco. '*Je vais vous assister*,' he said slowly, as though to a child. '*J'ai fait cette promesse à Madame Fabre.*' Or that's roughly what I caught.

Rebecca smiled too. Then she left the room so men could talk. It was like we were a part of some southern French Mafia. Despite my state, I couldn't keep the grin off my face—rage turned to warmth. Up till then I had entertained doubts about Renardo.

Lying in bed I was sure I was right about me. From what I could work out they'd want three things: the haul of forgeries—they had got them already, theirs to unload; the forger, they'd fixed things up in that department too (I didn't go along with the suicide theory); and thirdly, they wanted me because I knew too much, I had proved that already—proved it, in my innocence, to anyone who wanted to know. Proved it right from the moment I put the horses into the Beaulieu auction.

Renardo had seemed to understand that. Maybe that was why, when I got up from a bad sleep—even before sparrow's fart (if Feathers would forgive me)—there was a small man in a baggy tracksuit walking with Renardo on the lawn. In a sense it was Renardo's lawn, Aunt had written him into the house. Off-loading the house, in the terms of the will, I assumed, meant buying off the Pincis at a set figure.

Whoever's lawn it was they were walking on it and I was lying ill at ease with a .38 pistol under my pillow, the sort of thing I imagined would break your wrist if you didn't hold it in two hands.

If I had had the word 'Charge' surging around in my brain eight hours before, now it seemed that the charge had started leaving old Essington behind. The Pincis, Renardo and Rebecca, they had connections, but more than that I sensed through the fog of language that they had power. Renardo was like a *Parrain*, a Godfather. Maybe he'd always been doing just a little bit of business—moonlighting out of the Villa du Phare.

It's very quiet out in millionaire land early morning. There was no breeze, even the leaves were taking it easy, not bothering to fall.

A cat passed across Clyde's front steps, an action unthinkable before yesterday. I found myself picturing Clyde's empty house and all the full drawers inside it. I don't know why, I suppose I'd been struck by the neatness of everything.

I ate breakfast on my own, sitting in the sun for all the world to see; the picture of innocence. The odd car passed, but not a red car. The Bentley sat on the front drive; Renardo went over and over it with his chamois. He was not just playing a role; he liked the Bentley too much for that.

Nine-thirty. I walked inside and rang Dr Winter's number. Sophie answered. 'No, he isn't in yet, Essington.'

'Sophie, I know you're not going to like this.'

'Oh, God, Essington. You're still keeping on about the same things.'

'Sophie, two friends of mine got killed yesterday and the house next door was ransacked.' (I could hear Feathers: 'Hardly ransacked, Essington, that's hyperbole.')

'You're talking of those men who suicided. I read about it in this morning's paper.'

'It wasn't suicide. But I don't want to argue. Sophie, just leave a message for Dr Winter.'

'But you're not a client any more.'

'Don't worry about that, Sophie. Just tell him that I know who killed Thompson and Warner. Give him that message, will you? And Sophie, if you think I'm insane, watch the expression on his face and what he does next. In the end you'll see it my way.'

That should have been like sending up a flare.

I sat out the front again. Rebecca had removed the plate, the crumbs, the coffee-pot, the milk jug and the cup. All that remained was the .38 giving off a dull glow.

The man in the baggy tracksuit was lounging just inside the gate grill.

A curious silence fell over everything, more profound than the natural silence surrounding us. I could hear the telephone ring in the empty house next door. It rang a long time then rang out.

It would not have been my choice to sit like a painted wooden duck waiting to draw fire, but Renardo, blessed with the ability to withdraw into unbroken streams of the French language, had established ground rules as though this was to be a fight between the 'families'. He had produced the .38 from some mysterious cache. Maybe he had tactical nuclear warheads there as well: boxes of them in the woodshed.

Me, I would have headed straight down to the villa and got the bastards. And would I have been right? It seemed to me that hanging back allowed them time to get the pictures off, out of the country.

The man in the tracksuit was talking into a walkie-talkie.

Renardo polished the car.

The phone rang out a second time in Warner's house, the noise escaping through the smashed window.

Then Aunt's phone rang, was answered and Rebecca called to me through the open door.

'Holt?'

'Nice of you to call, Dr Winter.'

'I got some garbled message . . . people getting killed, threats . . . I choose to assume there is a confusion. There are, you understand, laws.'

'There's no threat. You've got that wrong. I was giving you information.'

'What do I want to know about dead nancy-boys?'

'What you want to know, Winter, is who killed them and, more important, who paid them to do it.'

'Why should I be interested in games? I'm a busy man.'

'Of course you are, you've got a lot of fake art to send off home.'

He hung up.

I rang his number. Sophie answered.

'Hello, it's me again, your loving friend, Essington.'

'Yes.'

'Could I speak to Dr Winter? He just hung up on me.'

'No you couldn't. He isn't in.'

'You gave him the message?'

'Yes.'

'And what was the expression on his face?'

'You are impossible. He had no expression. I gave it to him over the phone.'

'It got him to ring.'

'Did it?' Perhaps a note of uncertainty.

'Where from?'

'I couldn't say.'

'Thanks.' I hung up. She had to be lying her arse off.

Renardo had said that to get the hoods was just to get the hoods. Vengeance but nowhere. I'd got some vengeance since I'd been in France but still knew nothing for sure.

The phone rang again, before I was back out into the sunshine.

Chapter 22

'Essington?' It was Feathers. What the hell did he want?

'I've got some news that may interest you.'

'What time is it in Sydney?'

'If you must know, Essington, it's seven-fifteen, a bleak evening, coldest second November Wednesday since 1981.'

'Big deal.'

'There has been. Your friend Miles Jackson has just announced a coup. It actually makes newspaper headlines. A stack of French art. Purchased by a consortium of Australian businessmen to make up the core of the collection of the proposed Ayer's Rock Gallery. No details allowed but lots of confidential self-satisfaction. Remember the gallery . . . ? I sent a cutting, didn't I?'

'Feathers, the man who made those pictures was killed here yesterday.'

A long silence.

'They reproduced one of the paintings, a Seurat, nice-looking one; a study for a major work, they say.'

'Dr Winter, Feathers? How's he going with your partners?'

'They love him still, the blue-eyed boy . . . Dead, you say . . . How?'

'He got shot right through the head.'

'Do be careful, Essington. I'd better start digging deeper.'

'Do that.'

Plonk, and for half-way round the world a million miles of emptiness.

Just after I sat down again to stare fixedly at the gun, a car stopped outside the grill. Tracksuit was talking on his walkie-talkie and Renardo was cleaning the house side of the Bentley.

The gate opened, the car drove in, the gate shut. The car—a Renault panel van—drove up to Renardo. There was a conference.

Leave it to Renardo, Essington, Mr Wrong-About-Everything.

Those paintings had to have left France at least a week before. Warner had kept his side of the deal, telling no one. The thugs had simply been picking up the pieces, cleaning up.

But I was right about one thing, surely. They still had me to brush under the mat . . . me and Aunt's Degas. But if I was wrong about Winter . . . nobody else knew of the original monotypes except Grantley Simpson with the electric jug. He was beyond suspicion; that was where I'd put him. That was where I'd once put Jean-Pierre Thompson, put Winter—even Winter!

My brain hurt.

I didn't need psychology, I needed a psychologist. Annie? Heavens no!

I watched Renardo and the newcomer, engaged in earnest conversation.

Who were all these people? Was anyone on my side?

I thought of Karen, last seen on a subway train.

She just sort of was. The unknown happy wage-slave.

Karen actually had a sense of humour. If she'd seen over the edge she didn't care.

A prissy little bourgeois bitch like Sophie . . . she'd stick with Klaus Barbie if that was correct . . . but she wouldn't last two rounds with Karen.

Guarded by Mafiosi I was staring through trees at the Mediterranean Sea.

Was she, Karen, enjoying her view of the Pacific Highway? Grilling a chop?

Actually, I was missing my swim; each fine day potentially the last of a season determined to make it through to Christmas . . . Would have loved to be God, to be everywhere, to see what was happening at Villa Florida.

Renardo's visitor climbed back into the little van and drove down to the grill, it opened, shut, then off he purred, direction Beaulieu.

Renardo called me down from the terrace. I was pleased to move out of the firing-line, not that there was really anywhere to fire from.

The visitor had been doing some checking, working through connections at the administrative complex behind Nice Airport.

The Buick, deserted months ago facing the wrong way in a one-way street in the old port, was registered under Interwin Investments, Mt Boron. The address proved to be an unoccupied studio apartment in one of a jungle of new blocks with questionable sea-views. Checks revealed the apartment was owned by Erwin Consulting, registered at Monaco at the same address as the office of Dr Winter.

The car had been claimed the day after it was impounded, papers shown, fine paid by a flashy wiggly line that could have been one of Winter's signatures if you tried hard enough to decipher it. Yves had tried. Yves, I gathered, was our visitor in the Renault panel van.

Speaking slowly, with patience, Renardo got me to understand that the same car now sat in the drive of the Villa Florida: ubiquitous.

Who owned Villa Florida? It had been bought eighteen months ago for twelve million francs, by Interwin.

Eighteen months ago—I knew this from my morning economic readings to Aunt—the Australian dollar had been worth exactly twice its present value. Not a bad investment, doctor . . . a lot of grey matter behind the pebble glasses.

I could have kissed the ground they trod. Renardo and his messenger had given me the information I required to re-establish my near lost and always precarious self-esteem. The connection had been made. At last, positive proof: Winter was the man.

What an unruffled character the good doctor was. How inscrutable behind the camouflage of his glasses. Had it been that inscrutability which had caused me to mistrust my worst judgement of the man? Still, knowing what I knew of Winter was small comfort. Further down the line there were more important operators—like the man who went along as well when they visited Grantley Simpson at his cluttered London office.

I was pondering possible moves when an explosion, a rapid chain reaction, broke the tranquillity of the Cap. A flash of energy . . . tyres screamed . . . metal ripped metal. For an instant the rattle of gun-fire, then silence.

Renardo had thrown me to the ground behind the Bentley. He lay by my side, squinting along the barrel of an automatic shotgun

155

that must have lain in the car's shadow. He covered the gate . . . what was left of it.

All I could think of was that my .38, lying up on the table, was too far away. I stayed still.

Cautious, gripping the gun, still screened by the car, Renardo rose to a crouching position. Trembling, empty-handed, I followed his example. My gaze tracked with the gun's front sight as it panned the road beyond the drive. As though moved by a ghost, one of the Buick's doors swung open. Everything else was still. The other three doors hung wide, the car was askew on the bitumen, its nose buried into the side of a green Citroën delivery-van.

There was a figure slumped, bleeding, over the Buick's steering-wheel. As we approached I saw the front passenger pitched, face down, on to the roadway. He looked very dead, blood trickled from his open mouth. A gun had slipped out of his hand . . . just out of reach.

A third figure was crumpled about fifty metres back in the direction of the Villa Florida. He got his running away.

Our impenetrable steel grill was broken away from its catch by the initial blast. I learnt later it had been a grenade. A sub-machine-gun lay in the gutter, thrown by somebody, as though carelessly—the deadly toy that held no more interest.

I stood shocked, trembling. What was real? Had that im-measurably brief instant been a grotesque illusion?

So much death. Such vengeance.

I brought my body back under control. Stabilized, all I could consider was my fate had I followed first inclinations and hurried down to the Villa Florida—the wild colonial boy intent to even the score. Those professionals would have cut me to pieces.

Weirdly, there was nobody else alive in sight. We stood mid the carnage; Renardo's gun had vanished into thin air. And still no one as I caught the first, distant wail of sirens working up along the peninsula. Suddenly, like an echo, from down along the sea-walk, I heard two shots—clear and final. Then the first police car slid to a busy halt.

Beyond that moment only the hope of forgetting and endless hours of questions, hours of confusion and the long ride down to the *préfecture de police*.

When we had first ascended the steps to Aunt's door, the law in front, me behind, I noticed that the .38 had been removed from where it had basked like a lizard on my breakfast table.

Nobody, it seemed, owned the ancient Citroën van—it was out of registration. There would be little trouble following up the Buick. It turned out that it had been reported stolen only an hour before: tight planning.

Or that was what we were told at the *préfecture*.

Late afternoon a spear-fisherman snorkeling off the rocks by the lighthouse brought in the dead body of a clothed man bearing no papers. It was a man nobody had seen before. He was never identified. He had received two gunshot wounds to the head.

Renardo, the magician, conjured up a lawyer who did my talking for me and who seemed to mystify the already confused police with the varieties of his tortuous reasoning. This was Claude Chevet . . . if Renardo was Godfather was he an uncle?

By the time we got home it was late; I was stuffed, stuffed and grateful. Renardo had returned to the role of chauffeur as though we had lived no more than another day, one among the many. By mutual agreement we made no mention of the others, whoever they may have been. We had had one visitor that morning: Yves came to see Renardo. This, as the police in a post-revolutionary society well knew, was no concern of the master of the house.

· Renardo disappeared into the quarters he shared with Rebecca, unperturbed by the barking that accompanied our arrival. I was left on the terrace looking through the dark out on to what I saw, or imagined, as a silver sheet—the sea. (I always thought of it as ancient, the Mediterranean, as though the Pacific was some new-fangled gadget.) I wondered as we all must, even dogs I guess, about ideas of vastness, of light and sound and of how these bounce and how far they get.

The dog barked some more. I walked the villa's perimeter, to the rear yard. She was tied there, must have been returned through the afternoon. The Great Dane snarled low and dangerous.

'Leave it till morning, Essington,' I thought. 'A bit of tethering can do no harm.' Then I walked inside. One o'clock; if I was too tired I was also much too lonely. The aftermath of excitement—loneliness. Do we adventure only to tell the story? What had I said at school (picked, I guess because of my character, to be Othello when the English class read the play)? "My story being done,/She gave me for my pains a world of sighs:/She swore, in faith, 'twas strange, 'twas passing strange; 'Twas pitiful, 'twas wondrous pitiful.'"'

I had really taken to that role, Othello. Some comfort for despairing teachers? But I wasn't ready for the death scene. Not yet.

There was a number in my book of numbers, under 'P' for Polini. 'Karen?'

'Sorry, she's not here any more. Anyone else help you?'

'This is France. Have you got a number for her?'

'I think so, I'll look.'

'It costs a bomb.' The old poor Essington speaking.

'OK, I'll hurry.'

I was counting the seconds.

'Here it is: four-six-nine-two-eight-three.'

'Sydney?'

'Yep, Sydney.'

'Thanks.'

Nearly wears the finger out all the international dialling digits. By the time I got through to the three, I was starting to have second thoughts.

She picked up the phone on the second ring.

'Karen?'

'Essington?'

'No, it's General de Gaulle, how'd you guess?'

'Don't know, it just came. It's that voice . . . stagey.'

'What's the time, Karen?'

'Ten o'clock, you drunk?'

'No. France. Have you been burning candles for me?'

'At both ends.'

'Karen, I've been here for . . . Christ, must be more or less since we met. How's the Pacific Highway?'

'Oh, terrific. I'll hold the phone out so you can hear it.'

'And work? You changed jobs?'

'No, lost jobs. Steffano was an arsehole.'

'And his girl-friend . . . what's her name?'

'You've forgotten already? Annie.'

'Perfect bitch.'

'Your words.'

'Well, I love you, Karen. I just wanted to tell you.'

'That's sweet. I needed that. What time is it there?'

'It's around one o'clock and I've got stories to tell you to make your eyes spin.'

'Well, go on.'

'I've got to tell them here.'

'Forget it.'

'If I sent you a ticket would you come?'

'Tomorrow.'

'Might not be till the day after.'

'That's fine. I'm not booked up.'

'I mean it.'

'We'll see.'

'You will. Remember I love you.'

Then a long call to Feathers, a lot of which was Karen's ticket. I was a rich man, on paper at least. Time to learn the part.

Chapter 23

Animals like me, it's true. They like simple, uncomplicated old Essington. And I like animals, so it's mutual. You had to love the giant anyway, the vet had charged three thousand francs for the service.

It was a she, like the vet.

It watched as I approached. I carried my breakfast—coffee in one hand and a big chunk of bread in the other; the household had gone French. I sat at the extremity of the leash, sipping and dunking. She watched me, snarled—terrifying, the snarl—and watched me.

By mid-morning she'd eaten the bread and was walking on a choker. I called her Desdemona. It suited her. A beautiful creature. She sat between her legs like a sphinx, dead straight.

Rebecca wasn't so sure. It took more work with her than with the dog to get harmony in the household.

I'd been ringing Winter's office on the hour every hour. Sophie was getting chillier and chillier. And more and more worried. I suspected she wasn't making contact either.

Feathers rang. He wasn't getting anywhere because of the Winter fan club at the firm. But he had managed tickets for Karen and a blob of money transferred for me to keep the home fires burning.

The New Right was hailing the Alice Springs International Gallery project as yet another model of how the whole country could be rendered more effective. Gathering such a collection— now proudly and temporarily displayed in a Sydney private art-gallery—was a coup that showed what could be done once free enterprise was given its head.

'Free enterprise just killed all the fish in the Rhine, Feathers.'

'Yet, Essington, nobody owns shares in Chernobyl.'

Maybe he was right. Russia put together remarkable collections before the revolution. Even if peasants died in the winters.

I said, 'I'm liable to throw a spanner in the works.'

'Maybe you will, Essington. But maybe the works just won't accept the spanner.'

'Feathers, can you think of a man who could be involved; tough, thin hair, greying at the temples?'

Mid-afternoon, still no Winter.

'Sophie, you've got to face it. Surely you've had the police asking questions. Red cars owned by things like Interwin. Give up, for Christ's sake!'

But she'd prefer a straight little crook with a nice act any day. That's the French class system, I guess.

Late afternoon it was off for more chit-chat at the cop shop together with the unrufflable Mr Chevet who might have made it to my shoulder if he built up his built-up shoes. But couldn't the bastard talk a policeman under a table? No one was managing to connect me with anything or for that matter anything else with anything else.

I got back seven-thirty, maybe eight o'clock. Winter had rung and missed me. No number. He'd ring again before midnight.

Would he?

Rebecca's eyes flashed at Renardo, questioning.

'Renardo,' I said, 'this is just one man. I want to talk to him alone. I can handle him.'

He looked at Rebecca. What did she think? his expression demanded.

She shrugged, dropping a tight black plait further down between her shoulder blades as she poured wine over slithers of veal simmering in a pan.

I ate in solemn silence. Waiting to hear the ring. Desdemona sat attentive at my feet; looking up, watching. Someone had trained that dog before Clyde bought it. Trained it as a weapon of defence. It was responding to my constant checks and commands.

I had thanked Renardo for his help. Since then, by mutual consent, we said nothing—back in our places. The same pattern as when the house was under the rule of Aunt Eloise, only the food had changed. And I felt uninhibited about entering the kitchen area, legacy of French conversation lessons abandoned in the action of the last few days.

I still had to break the news about Karen. I was not sure I knew what she looked like. She was little more than a person I had last seen in a crowded train.

The phone rang. I let it go four, five rings, picked it up.

'Holt?'

'Yep.'

Renardo slipped in the door, stood and watched.

Desdemona was on her feet, frozen, like she was made of ceramic.

'Listen.'

'Don't tell me to listen, pop-eyes. You're on a losing streak, remember.'

'See it your way, anyway you like. We've got to talk. There's a lot of problems, a lot of misunderstandings.'

'Drop around, Winter. We're living in a civilized world.'

'I'd rather you came to see me.'

'I can't see what we've got to talk about. I tried talk already. You're a brick wall.'

The dog popped its haunches on the floor and kept on staring at my head, working out what I was doing talking into a plastic bone.

'I don't know what you're trying to say.'

'Four guys came here yesterday in your car . . . they were a death squad, Winter. You've been turning up the heat . . . but watch it, we'll see who gets burned.' An empty threat, perhaps.

Renardo walked across the room, took the phone out of my hand, hung it up. Desdemona leapt at him but stopped on a loud command, just short of his arm.

Renardo smiled, shook his head. 'It's not good to talk too long.'

'Renardo, can we go for a drive?'

He shrugged his shoulders. 'Why not?'

The little Renault van was parked outside the Villa Florida down the road. Renardo had a word with the driver. Nobody had come or gone. The villa was empty.

We tried the office address at Monaco after doing a Brabham

round the Corniche in the Bentley. Nothing there either. He could have been anywhere. In some hotel from Toulon to Menton. There were thousands of them.

And what could he have hoped for by contacting me? A cathartic confession? Or a final crack at knocking me off?

Me? For me he was the last lead into the Australian connection. I was starting to form a picture of that connection in my primitive mind. There'd be no way right in without Winter.

We returned past Cap Ferrat and tried the address of the Interwin apartment on Mt Boron. No Winter in the gloomy block of concrete.

It was late. We drove down into Villefranche to take a coffee on the quai. There were three or four couples at the open café, braving night chills for ambience and for the soft strumming of a Carioca singer with an eager little rhythm player tapping anything he could get his hands on. All the tunes sounded the same—sure touchstone of Brazilian quality.

Renardo tired of my attempts at conversation. We sat in silence. The proprietor came out and sat next to him. I received the serious man-to-man handshake. Then they had things to discuss, that was clear enough.

Desdemona was beneath the table watching me, with an occasional glance at the musicians; twitching an ear, maybe, if the note changed by more than a semitone at a time.

Jesus it was beautiful, the bay. No United States destroyers in sight. I expect they were cruising just outside Colonel Qaddafi's territorial waters to keep the rest of us glued to the edge of our seats. In their place a couple of middle-sized ships, part of the Mediterranean tourist trade, their rows of party lights shining. Behind them, nestling just off the Plage de Passable, a cluster of pleasure boats still braving waters to which winter was soon to arrive—last year it snowed in Nice and the eucalyptus trees were still looking pretty bashed about by the experience.

Watching the beauty of all this and lulled by the gentle undulations of the music, I failed at first to register the cruiser lying off the Villa Florida. It had seemed part of a general night boatscape. But no. When I focused on it, it was closer, clearly moored off the point. And there was a light in the cabin, much dimmer than the mooring lights and thus not initially apparent.

I mentioned to Renardo that I would walk along the beach to the point and leave him to his conversation. He could drive down and pick me up when he was ready. If I wasn't there, wait. I'd turn up.

I put Desdemona into the Bentley. She looked at home inside, watching me set off along the sea wall above the sand—the right dog for the right car.

I swam out to the boat. There was the name, *Sydney Dreaming*—Nicholls' cruiser, his Guernsey bargain. I climbed the stern ladder. There was no sound inside but he had to be on board, the dinghy was tethered at the stern, bobbing in counterpoint.

Through a cabin window I could see Winter bent over a table, writing. He was surrounded by little piles of paper, by files, by the yellow glow of the light. He had a shotgun resting like a long paperweight across the desk. What a creepy little bastard, blinking at figures through the windows that brought them into focus.

I thumped on the roof.

Startled, he leapt to his feet grabbing the gun. Suddenly a lonely figure turning slowly about, watching the circle of windows holding back the night. He went towards the door that led, via steps, to the deck; but he was indecisive. He returned to the centre of the room.

All you could hear was the lapping of water and the little scuffly mouse-like noises of Winter.

It was a sizeable boat; if he went further in, up forward, he'd be hard to get at. He could sit up there with a gun and pump it empty of shells at whoever and whatever approached. They hold a lot of cartridges those automatic shotguns.

He settled down again.

The windows were sliding glass panels; shut, most of them. I worked my way around to one left open—a narrow slit for air to slide through.

'Winter.' Whispered.

He was up again like a shot, circling with his gun.

'Put it down or I'll blow your brains out.'

'Holt.'

'Put the fucker down. I don't want to kill you. I want to talk.'

Click. Click. Click. Click. Click. You could hear the gears turning round in his head. He'd clutch the gun, half-raise it to his shoulder, nearly put it down.

'When I get to ten, Winter, it's hello God!

'One . . . two . . . three.' He was like a rabbit while a warren's being dug from all holes at once.

'Four . . . Renardo, don't shoot till I tell you.' Bluffing that I was not alone.

'Five . . .'

By the time I reached seven he was spinning like a wheel, hands clutched over his ears. And screaming.

'Nine . . . Winter, ten . . . Hold it Renardo . . . for God's sake hold it. Winter, keep your hands on your head. Nod if you can hear me.'

He nodded.

'Keep them there . . . that's right. Now walk slow . . . hands high, that's nice, up the steps . . . good . . . out the door . . .'

He came out. I grabbed him, ripped the glasses off and hurled them into the water.

'I can't see, I can't see anything.'

I hauled him back into the cabin. Sat him down, put the gun out of reach. 'Now, tell me about it.'

When I waded back into the beach Renardo was standing up on the road by the Bentley.

The dog came running as though we had grown up together. I patted her head and she sat, instantly content. I hovered, draining, jogging on the spot, keeping warm.

Renardo came with a rug from the boot of the car. He bent down, picked up the little pile of my clothes. Then we heard it, one shot. It had taken Winter a long time to find the gun.

'Quelle heure est-il, Renardo?'

It was just before midnight. Karen would be waiting for a taxi. Or maybe she'd have the luck to go down to the airport in Feathers' natty car. Roaring along slowly—too slowly if you wanted to get anywhere, and I hoped she did.

For conversation I tried to say to Renardo, as we wound our

way up and out of the lanes of Villefranche, that Mr Chevet would have even more talking to do now. But I don't know if I made myself understood.

Drinking a brandy, standing observing the now familiar view—familiar night and day—I found myself wondering about what had happened to me. Winter dead. I felt nothing—nothing. Maybe I shuddered once but that was at the image of the bang, what all those pellets would do to his head at that range. Compassion? Not a touch.

Well, not for Winter but, curiously, more for the four hired hands who had walked into Renardo's ambush. They were like all the little soldiers who fill the world's spare paddocks while the Winters work out some new game for them to play. There was satisfaction to be had from Winter going down the plug hole after them.

What would they talk about in hell?

Desdemona sat and watched me. Did she know that we had avenged the death of her . . . surely her brother, altogether a braver and less wise dog.

Chapter 24

About the time when Karen would have been taking off I was dreaming that I was very small and something very big was trying to pick me up in its grasping hand. I was dodging when I fell. My body gave a leap. I was awake, lying in the quiet, the dark, the oscillation of the lighthouse beam.

By the time she would have been flying out over the Timor Sea, heading for Jakarta, I was taking breakfast, sharing it with Desdemona in the sun—thick aromatic coffee, hot milk, *baguette*, *confiture*. Very European. I was uncertain about the passing of bacon and eggs from the morning table; tea was no loss at all.

I rang Feathers who gave me a brief description of the departure and details like flight numbers, arrival times, the colour of her eyes. Only on reflection did I realize that I was importing someone who was almost a stranger.

'Beautiful, I dare say, Essington. If a fraction rough-hewn, a fraction wild.'

'She laughs, Feathers. That's a rare thing in your po-faced world. You know what I reckon? She might even have a soul. That would be a change . . . a soul. Like a carry-over from some earlier stage.'

'Indeed, a rare thing.'

'So, how are things at Grimbole and Curly?'

'Richards and Temple, Essington. Curious would still be the word I think. I'm afraid that you have set off a chain of action–reaction. God knows who will finish up getting hurt.'

'You've been digging?'

'Deep, Essington. Too deep, I'm beginning to fear.'

'Then write, let me in on it. I can't hang here nattering over the phone. It costs money, Feathers.'

'Think of it as business. The cost comes off your tax.'

'My tax?'

'By-product of ill-gotten wealth. There will be a substantial tax bill on the earnings of your inheritance. Talking to your solicitor is a deduction, Essington.'

Details like that were going to take me a long time to digest. The previous year I had earned so little I had not qualified to pay tax. Let alone fiddle deductions.

'Well, watch your neck, Feathers. The chain reaction got to you yet?'

'Fire smouldering round my feet.'

'So watch out it doesn't catch the wind. I've been thinking all this over—the business side, your side. I put it together with what I managed to extract from Dr Winter. Those guys . . . they are too far in. They will stop at nothing. Too much at stake, Feathers. Not only money, like your honest criminal; it's big business. And there's the whole charade of respectability to be kept up. I don't know how things stand right now but when I left there was a lot of double talk about nationalism, paying your taxes like a good chap, building a better Australia. Avoiding your dues was suddenly a no-no. OK, they still did it, but no talk of it over dinner, not any more.'

He interrupted my eloquence: 'Winter told you . . . you said?'

'Sure did. The details. The whole box and dice. Tell me, could you do one thing for me, for your old cobber? Could you send me a picture of your Temple, of Richards' better half?'

'Temple?' he asked. 'But why on earth, Temple?'

'Feathers, I know you're not going to like this but . . . well, I think I love that guy. I want to have his face under my pillow.'

'But Temple, implicated . . . It just couldn't be possible. Wouldn't make sense. No sense at all.'

'What does? Take it from me, your Winter was guilty as hell; hands covered in blood.'

'Hyperbole, Essington.'

'Crap! Real blood, real hands, even if by extension. And you vouched for him.'

'Whatever your claim, Temple's untouchable.' There was a pause. I could feel the international meter ticking away while Feathers did his thinking. 'Unless,' he continued, 'someone like Winter . . .'

'No chance with the good doctor, he's gone incommunicado.'

'Oh!'

'Feathers, down here it's been like a re-enactment of the 1944 invasion. If you didn't duck you got hit.'

'And you ducked?'

'I crawled on my stomach, Feathers. By the way, you couldn't send the catalogue of the Miles Jackson art extravaganza if there is one? I'd be interested. And the Temple photo. If only to clear his name this end.'

Lunch, I chomped away on a *pain beignet* at a little bar on the walk above the Villefranche beach. Karen would have been heading over India. Desdemona lay quiet at my feet. I could watch the launch, *Sydney Dreaming*, ride at her anchor. Could be days, even weeks, before anyone bothered to take a look. That was unless the Nichollses got to miss it.

'Desdemona,' I said, patting the great peaceful head, 'she'll be eating through her four millionth pack of food by now.'

The hound wagged her tail once.

By the time I made a slightly dizzy return around the coast, balance diminished by sun and wine, the flight from Sydney would have been in sight of the fires marking the oil fields of the Middle East.

I hardly slept.

Two o'clock the next afternoon I stood at Nice airport examining the faces as they filed off the flight from Paris. I recognized her by a process of elimination. And then, close up, by the smile she tried out to see if it was me. We were lost people finding each other.

'Karen?'

'That's the voice,' she said. 'Mr Elocution.'

Being thrown on to the heap of the unemployed had transformed her into a creature of her own fantasy. An exquisite fantasy. No more the secretary. I had seen women got up like that before, but not along the Côte d'Azur. I had seen them on the TV, in coverage of Paris fashion parades—the *Prêt-à-Porter* in the Tuileries Gardens. Magic names: Kenzo, Koshino, Miyake, Gautier; the self as a work of art. Karen had, to my eyes at least, outdone them all. Her hair, pale apricot darkening at the tips, framed a face fresh from the light of the Pacific. Plaited multi-coloured tails hung down behind. She looked tired, drawn, from the flight. But even that couldn't suppress the gaiety. She was dressed à la mode for that European autumn and winter—black on black on black.

'Karen,' I repeated, clasping her hands then stepping back for an examination.

'What do you think?' she asked. 'The lady of leisure.'

'Leisure! We've got floors to scrub.'

'You scrub, Mr Holt. I'll watch.'

We kissed.

'Isn't it romantic? But remember, Essington, we only met once.' She stepped out of my embrace. 'Hey! You forgot to tether your horse.'

'Horse? Oh, Jesus! I forgot. Karen, this is Desdemona . . . she's been keeping me warm while you've been gone.'

The crowd couldn't wait to get through and off to their high-rise concrete dreams. By the time I emerged from my trance it was just the two of us, a few officials and those whose nearest and dearest had missed the plane. Karen was kneeling, holding the dog by the ears.

'Luggage?' I asked.

'That's it, the cabin bag. I hurled the rest out. I am the new me—globe-trotter *extraordinaire*. It's a movie, Essington. It's in the script.'

We walked out to the car park.

'No taxi? Essington, you've got wheels? The steering-wheel on the wrong side and everything?'

'More than wheels, Karen.'

I had argued Renardo into using the hat for once. 'Just for the theatre,' I suggested. I guess he suspected I had my vulgar side. But then, if you've got it, stick to it—that's the rule.

Karen was not going to be surprised by anything.

Renardo took the bag, put it in the boot. Looked around for more.

'It looks nice, lovely colour yellow. But does it go?'

'Like the wind.'

'And I had you picked for a scrag. Your light . . . why it must have been under a bushel and a half.'

'My light, Karen, wasn't even lit till five minutes ago.'

It was obvious that Rebecca couldn't wait to see what the cat dragged in. She was the welcoming committee at the top of the steps; beaming, arms folded over her ample bosom. The Bentley slid to a halt, crunching the gravel.

When Karen stepped out Rebecca's smile faltered, then became fixed. What had she expected? Grace Kelly? Somebody cast in an earlier mould?

We climbed the steps; Renardo brought up the rear, underladen. 'You should have brought at least one large suitcase . . . even if you'd loaded it with bricks. Appearance is everything in Europe.'

But then so is effect.

Karen had saved the best up for last. She held out a hand to Rebecca: '*Bonjour Madame.*' Then she was off, chatting like a member of the French Secret Service returned from a scuba-diving holiday in New Zealand.

Rebecca couldn't keep the smile down after that.

Later I asked: 'How d'you do it, Karen?'

'Tongues.'

'No, really?'

'My father, Essington, mixed-blood. I was born in New Caledonia. But my mother's Australian. We moved to Brisbane when I was seven. The Australian wife as a ticket to the economic wonderland; that's the New Caledonian dream.'

'How long ago was that?'

'Five years—I'm twelve. You remember that now. My sexual integrity is protected by law for the next four years. You may, if you so desire, hold my hand . . . but not too hard.'

We were standing in the middle of the vast room that Rebecca, in the interests of a respectable house, had prepared for our guest. The shutters were open, sunlight flooded over waxed parquetry and the sumptuous reds and blues of Persian rugs.

'Tired?' I asked.

'Where did you get all the money from?'

'Not tired?'

'No. Even a little frisky.'

'Then. . . ?'

She began to peel off layers of black, revealing, little by little, pale tanned skin—legacy of Sydney sunshine.

The dinghy tethered at the stern of *Sydney Dreaming* was nuzzling against the cruiser's hull like a calf. The thought of the cabin's contents adversely affected my appetite as Karen and I sat at a table outside Pellegrini's, gobbling down our bouillabaisse among a throng of aged Monaco day-trippers. We were already becoming settled with each other, getting about like any old honeymoon couple.

I had been forced to unload a portion of the burden on my soul after Karen had been confronted and questioned by police a couple of days after her arrival. They had come to the villa still searching out connections between seemingly unconnected events. The lawyer, Chevet, continued to practise the mysterious logic of his craft and to keep me out of the law's hands.

While filling Karen in on what had happened I had skipped over those of my activities that seemed to reflect badly upon me; that revealed the more brutal side of my character. To tell the truth I had been labouring to obscure the same actions from myself so that they might sink beneath consciousness.

And there I was with the bouillabaisse and the launch that was determined to haunt my mind. Days before, I had entertained the idea of scuttling her where she was anchored, but then thought better of it. The way to establish a distance between *Sydney Dreaming* and myself was to keep that distance.

It's a messy eat, the seafood in all that soup. The catalogue which had arrived in that morning's mail was already splashed with the juices. Clyde Warner's beautiful mock Seurat, the study for the *Models in the Studio*, was smeared.

Although interested in my story, Karen found little to hold her attention in the catalogue reproductions. Even my Rodins were disregarded. Me, I thought them pretty convincing, found myself turning back to their page with secret pride. A celebrated scholar had climbed down out of his ivory tower, put pen to paper and sung their praises in a jumble of phrases and words. Those Rodins were for him representatives of the essence of 'inter-gender reciprocity within the matrix of broader socio-economic parameters'.

'Essington . . . what's he trying to say?'

'Nothing. Just holding down a job.'

'I guess that's his problem then.' She flipped a few pages. 'Those ones;' she was pointing at two of the Degas. 'They're the ones up in the house, aren't they?'

'There're six.'

'So, isn't it a problem then . . . you having them as well? Proves theirs are fakes.'

'Not if everyone wants to believe in what Jackson's got, it doesn't.'

'They wouldn't believe you?'

'Why should they? I'd just seem pissed off, wouldn't I? Years ago my aunt was had . . . stiff cheese. Nobody to do with her deal exists any more. They came with a whole box of photos . . . They don't exist either.'

'Pity,' she said. 'They would have been interesting, the photos. I love photos. Curious, those monotypes look better to me than anything else they've got. Maybe because they look a bit like photos—the greys, the format.'

'And how about these drawings?' I opened the catalogue at a particularly explicit Rodin—legs apart, a couple of lines representing the vulva.

'They're just lines. I don't go so much for your modern art. That's why I prefer photos. They show what things look like.' She was extracting the flesh of some hapless sea-creature from its shell. No, a messy meal to eat.

'Essington, how about that man in London? You said he'd know. It was him who identified your aunt's Degas as fakes in the first place, wasn't it?' Karen smiled vacantly at the gulls edging towards the tables in search of food. But she wasn't being vacant. 'So, why don't you get him to come over here and have a look?'

The ace of hearts had just popped out of my sleeve. Of course, the answer: Grantley Simpson. To be a Degas a picture had to be a Simpson-approved Degas.

Then she was leaning forward. Her eyes had narrowed. 'He knocks off six of them, declares them fake, then people will have to listen about all the rest, won't they?' She flipped the book over. 'What does it say here at the start?' The more she handled it the more spoilt the catalogue became. 'There . . . that piece by the Right Honourable Thingummybob. See, there . . . "valued conservatively at fifty million dollars." That's a lot of taxable income to lose, isn't it? Even worse to find that you've got it back again.'

'You mean you understand all that stuff?'

'Sure, Essington. Nothing to understand really.'

I had a vague notion of how tax incentives worked—the deductions with the pot of gold at the end. I had more or less followed what Winter had been explaining to the Armitages and the Nichollses during the meal in what now felt like another era. I guess I failed to concentrate on the detail because my mind had never been called on to work that way.

Karen made it clear as daylight. Just before the end of a financial year, that was just before June 30, those with the good fortune to earn a heap of money hunt around for somewhere to put it, to shelter it from the tax man. A farmer might buy a lot of fencing materials the cost of which can be deducted from taxable income. I remembered that from rural days, the flurry of buying late in June. If you bought the stuff in July that could only be claimed against the next year's income. So, if you made a killing in a financial year, you had to chalk up deductions against that killing in the same year. Balls that up and you paid out a slab of tax. If these things were managed right a year of unusually high income could be turned into a benefit for future years. Thus the fencing materials could be used over subsequent years of meagre earnings.

The art deal Winter had talked about made it possible to give away paintings and deduct their value from taxable income. If you purchased a picture thirty years earlier it might have acquired sufficient value to wipe out tax liability in the year you make your killing. And the nation's happy because they get a valuable work of art.

Simpson and I had got along all right. It was no trouble at all to entice him down to the Mediterranean. Anyway, he needed the money; well, that would have been my guess. He was at Nice the next day.

174

We did Degas first. Each monotype was extracted from its frame before being subjected to careful examination. He had a little magnifying glass that he pulled out of a cardigan pocket. This he ran over the paper's surface missing contact by a hair's-breadth. He made clicking noises with his tongue. Rebecca brought up tray after tray of tea; maybe too weak for the connoisseur. Actually, Grantley had approved the set at first glance. The inspection was to justify the fee and air fare. Dandruff dropping out of his hair must have done the monotypes as much damage as the previous hundred years of life's vicissitudes. If the old Degas fanatic had changed clothes for the trip I would have been pushed to nominate which ones. Somehow, out of his office, he looked even shabbier. Karen, being the well-washed Australian, was acutely sensitive to his odour of dust and body.

'Oh! No, no,' he muttered to himself. 'Oh, excellent, excellent. Quite a discovery. Oh, but I will regret your aunt's photographs to my dying day.'

'She did, I can assure you, Mr Simpson.'

He straightened up letting out a little involuntary cry of pain as his back moved from one familiar position to another. 'Lovely, simply lovely. See what wit he had. Of course, you know, he had it in his daily life as well. The master of the interior, it was Degas who pointed out that painting is not a sport, therefore it should not be done outdoors. He was supreme, such facility, such observation. It will never come again. It was a moment.' Simpson turned to Karen who had been observing him with a mixture of fascination and distaste. There were tears welling up behind his specs. He had become positively red-eyed.

'I would like you to consider, each of you, the immensity of time . . . dimensionless. And somewhere in all that ether, Degas. Nothing runs in circles. That is metaphysical poppycock. History has no form. We do not go from anywhere to anywhere. Eternity is built of moments. Degas was a brilliant moment.'

Grantley Simpson stayed with us for three days during which Renardo chauffeured him about to see items on a check-list of loved objects. He showed me the list. When he saw something he ran a line through its name. The true scholar.

I showed him the photograph that Feathers had included with

the catalogue. It was a head shot of Temple. 'That's the one,' Grantley exclaimed without so much as a second thought: a trained observer. 'That's him . . . came to me with the picture to verify, with the Degas monotype; the copy of one of yours. There were two of them; that was the arrogant one.'

Feathers had written what he had worked out of the story from his perspective. Temple had masterminded the scheme in consultation with Miles Jackson. Then they marketed it to a group of investors with tax problems. Temple got a percentage as his fee; well, it went to the firm. Had he also participated in the tax-avoidance angle?

The idea of the Ayers Rock Gallery had been openly promoted among a section of Sydney's business community by both Jackson and Temple. Nothing clandestine about that. From what Feathers could make out, even viewed in its least favourable light, all that the scheme involved was the striking of valuations well above purchase price. Nothing so remarkable about that either; it was an imperfect world. The valuation would be high enough to provide marginal tax advantages, but the principal attraction seemed to be the glory of an association with the establishment of the new gallery near the great rock at Australia's centre.

He wrote: 'Essington, I am led to understand that there are a considerable number of paintings involved. This is substantiated by the catalogue. The purchase price was negotiated with an allowance being made for the magnitude of the deal as a whole. To sell so many pictures singly would take time. Their simultaneous appearance on the market would undercut their individual value as there are a finite number of buyers at any given time. Thus, valued separately, their combined value would be considerably higher than the negotiated purchase price.'

He went on to detail fluctuations in the value of the Australian dollar, and features of the hedging mechanisms of the Futures Market which enabled people trading from one currency to another to protect themselves against a sudden fall in the value of the money they were obliged to use. It was over my head. All I could glean was that it further increased their profits.

'In addition, Essington, the market has proved itself to be on

176

the side of Temple and Jackson's scheme. You are no doubt aware of the sale of a smallish Manet for approximately seventeen million Australian dollars and the more recent Van Gogh *Sunflowers* topping fifty-five million. Who, in such a climate, would query fifty million for a collection of little gems? I fear your overactive imagination may be colouring your judgement. Our Mr Temple has been inventive, yes; criminal, absolutely not.'

So, I asked myself, why the killing?

Because, the pictures were fake. They cost . . . not even the fee arranged with Jean-Pierre. I felt certain that it had been the forger's dealer who was heavied at the start.

A fifty-million-dollar tax deduction—representing a saving of around twenty-five million dollars at the top tax rate—all for the cost of a hit man. How much to get someone killed? I didn't know. I had never felt the need . . . well, not to employ anyone for it anyway.

And then another question came to mind. Had they intended the killings right from the start? Or had Clyde Warner and Jean-Pierre Thompson died because I happened along? Had I got in the way? Confused the plan? Or had I simply generated a second wave of thought?

'Christ! He's written a lot of books.' Karen was thumbing through my tome on Degas's graphic works.

'Who?'

'In this bibliography . . . your smelly friend, the tea drinker. One, two . . .' her finger sliding down the page. 'Only eleven, Essington.'

'Give me a look.' Sure enough there they were, listed. A number must have been catalogue notes or booklets. There just wouldn't have been the market.

We were settled among breakfast crumbs on the terrace. Rebecca came to see if we needed more coffee. Karen leapt to her feet, assisting, prattling away in French.

Once we were alone I put in a word in the interests of domestic harmony. Rebecca had weathered a lot of changes in a short time. I had taken over from Aunt, then the arrival of Desdemona on the scene, and finally, Karen. Not to mention the constant and persistent intrusions of the law. 'She thinks you're trying to displace her, Karen. There's no need to help. It's her job. She gets paid. So does Renardo. That's why he drives us around the place. With you jumping up and down like God knows what we're liable to finish up with a demarcation dispute.'

I was ignored for my trouble. Karen continued flicking over the pages of the Degas book with absolutely no sign of interest in its contents. Thin clouds were drifting across from Africa. Renardo arrived with the *Herald Tribune* headlining the second largest bank in the United States with iiquidity problems.

Wind and increasing cloud forced us out of the printed word and back to each other. Karen had closed the book. She was staring at the dull blue-grey sea while sucking her bottom lip. She was picking an ear with her little finger. 'Essington?'

She made me nervous. Maybe I thought of her as almost too beautiful. Certainly too beautiful for me, for the ageing Essington. Would she, one day, simply up and go? Do an Annie? Not that I had any regrets in that department.

'I have been thinking,' she announced.

That was what I had been afraid of. 'Karen . . .' I wanted to get in first. 'We could take a trip. If you want we could go over to London for Christmas. Holly; the poor dying in the streets.'

'Why should I want to go to London for Christmas? That's the Mediterranean out there . . . plastic bags and all. It's a one-off, an original. Mythic, Essington. Anyway, I like it here.'

I smiled all over my face. 'You've been thinking?'

'Believe it or not.'

'Oh! I do, I do, I assure you, Karen.'

'Well, firstly, tell me the rest about the fake pictures . . . about the man next door. All about everything. This time the lot. I want to know.'

Chapter 25

It was getting colder by the minute. As though the cloud from over Africa had an appointment with a wind driving down from the snow at our backs—from the French ski-fields. We retreated inside. Desdemona trotted attentively at my side; very much a one-man dog.

I led the way to the dressing-room where the Degas hung. That seemed the most appropriate place to deliver the uncut version. Under the gaze of those naughty ladies and their gentlemen, under their bona fide Degas gaze, I laid the story out piece by piece. Finally we headed down to the laundry where I went through the actions of printing a monotype. I showed her the Cibachromes. She thumbed through the bouillabaissed Jackson catalogue.

'And you did those?' Pointing at the Rodins.

'Thinking of you.'

'I'll bet. And they're hanging in Sydney? I like it. It's wonderful.' Suddenly the whole thing had arrested her interest.

'Not so wonderful once you think of all the other stuff in Australian public collections that may not stand close examination. Anyway . . . you hated my Rodins, remember?'

'But the whole thing . . . I love it. And what else?'

'The horses. I did the horses, the last one.' We were making our way upstairs.

She flipped the pages. 'Not too bad, Mr da Vinci Holt.'

That far into the story I had avoided death. Its memory returned as a reaction to the levity we were sharing over my criminal complicity.

'It wasn't just Jean-Pierre and Clyde who got killed, Karen.'

Catching my tone she closed the catalogue. 'Go on.'

I told her of Renardo's massacre. She walked to a gilded Empire chair which creaked as she slumped into it. She stared out through the window at the greying world. 'And?' she asked.

179

Well, there was still Winter and the boat; I told her about that. 'Jesus Christ! He's still there?'

'It's all I can see when I'm over that side.'

She went blank. I fidgeted with the Cibachromes, shuffling them over and over. It was nasty, all of it. Would it stick? Like Mark Antony or Caesar or Herod or whoever . . . would it wash off? Would my hands come clean?

I broke the silence. 'A great big fibreglass coffin with hot and cold running water.'

'You're telling the truth, aren't you, Essington?'

'The whole of it.'

She walked over, stood on my toes, reached up and grabbed me by the ears, like I was Desdemona. She kissed me as she might a child who's lost something. 'You poor bastard. And I thought you'd been having fun.'

'That's what I thought at the start.'

Staring at me, examining. I could see concern plucking at the muscles around her eyes. 'Oh . . . Essington.'

I dropped my head into her hair to disguise welling tears—gratitude and, I guess, a little self-pity.

That moment was a kind of turning-point for Karen and me. And it was also the time she took over the thinking. She had the mind for it. For how to bring the bastards down. I had considered it every which way. Always drawing a blank. Action was what I could do—but from half-way round the world? Karen conceived a plan. She knew the arithmetic, the timing.

Mid-afternoon I rang Winter's office. Sophie answered. She was stiffer, less communicative than usual. Winter was out of the country for several days. Did she believe it? Could she take a message? Piss off, Essington Holt.

When Karen rang the same number she got the same message, only in French.

Next I wrote Winter a letter in which I explained that I would like to apologize for earlier misunderstandings. My confusion had been on account of Aunt's illness, unfamiliar surroundings and so on. Could we get together, make up over a meal. I owed it to him. Maybe he would like to bring the charming Mlle Vaujour.

That got posted. So, I believed Winter alive and well.

Nicholls and his wife would only be too happy to join us for lunch the next day. We would meet at Pellegrini's, a table booked in my name.

It was as though Karen was playing chess. I guess she'd moved out a couple of pawns. The way she saw it Temple and his mates could only get caught if trapped publicly. They had too much clout otherwise. Who would believe a word uttered by one Essington Holt, who had once accepted a painting as a bribe to stop bidding at an auction; who was so small-time he hardly paid tax, let alone knew of ways around it.

Patience. Karen preached patience. If they were to be trapped publicly it had to be later rather than sooner.

'Give them time to come out of the woodwork, Essington.'

'Or to bury themselves completely.'

'They won't do that. Why should they do that?'

'Because, Karen, I still exist. It's still possible for me to blow the whistle.'

'That's just it, you can't. Nobody's going to believe you about anything. You're the little guy. What's more, the longer you stay quiet, the surer they'll be that they are in the clear.'

'Or they send someone to wipe the slate clean, to bump me off.'

'Why should they? They haven't yet. You said you thought the dirty stuff was Winter's department. That phase is finished. Those people, they are happy, celebrating. They have the lot. The pictures are already on display, chalking up credits. Evidence: the catalogue. Jackson's come out, declared himself. Essington, I promise you, only give them time.'

Then she moved her first big piece. That was a bit I liked; Grantley Simpson.

What she worked out was to prevail upon him to prepare a French translation of a text already published—but fifteen years ago—under the title *Degas, Graphic Works: A Definitive Catalogue Raisonné*. He would get paid—maybe the book would sell. Why should he refuse? The rider was that Aunt's six monotypes were to be added. Added and illustrated.

'Maybe a paragraph or two additional to the original introduc-

181

tion. If Grantley Simpson is the man you say he is, Essington, publishing that book will be like planting a bomb. Only, with the catalogue, no innocent bystanders get hurt. It would prove their monotypes were fakes.'

'And?' I asked.

'And, bonehead, you've got the real ones, haven't you? People are going to want to talk to you. You'll become the centre of attraction. By publishing you blow the whistle on the lot, on their whole collection. The only thing is, Essington, it has to be right at the end of the financial year. So they're stuck with the claim against taxable income. That way, it doesn't matter who or what they are, if they get prosecuted or not, at the very least they lose their money. And it's a lot of money to lose . . . not to mention loss of face.'

I got so I couldn't think about it at all. It went so much against my grain. It seemed like fighting somebody by running in the opposite direction. Or fighting nothing, thin air—like sparring in a vacuum. Aunt had tried to teach me to go slow, to use my head. But what Karen was doing was ridiculous. What, I wondered, would the old woman have thought of Karen?

Whenever that question entered my mind I got the same answer. She would have approved. I shut up and did what I was told.

Not without some resistance. 'And who pays for the book?' I asked.

'Why, you do, of course. Who knows, you might even sell a few. If those pictures of yours are worth what you claim then you might as well make sure that the whole world knows which are the real ones. It's money well invested.'

I bashed a letter off to Grantley offering a deal and requesting that he think about a suitable publisher. When I got to think about it, Karen was using a technique not unlike that of Temple and the boys. She was using the public arena, public approval, to make her point.

'How did you learn to do all this, Karen?'

She laughed: 'Steffano, your old friend, he was into everything.'

'I found that out.'

'Financially as well. Every fancy tax scheme he could get his hands on. He was a sucker for them. Around tax time brochures flooded the mail; mostly shonky deals of one kind or another. I made a study of them. They interested me. Steffano liked film investment best. You put in a thousand, you were allowed to claim one thousand three hundred off taxable income. I think he figured it was a way to get among the starlets.'

'No starlets now, with Annie about.'

'You never know. Maybe she'd be on to them too.'

Feathers' policy was peace at all costs. I guess that was how he got to be a partner in the first place. His corporation could not accept the idea of Richards and Temple being involved in violent crime. (He even used the word 'we' when talking about the firm.) As far as he was concerned, if there had been heavy stuff it occurred at the French end—where the foreigners were. OK, Temple might be implicated in the tax fraud but . . . maybe, in Sydney, there weren't many 'haves' who weren't. His attitude suited Karen. Feathers had been the weakest point as far as she was concerned. Too much snooping about on his part and the lid could blow off, prematurely.

He had taken to ringing. Too often. Perhaps he was worried. Perhaps he was fishing on Temple's behalf.

As instructed, I was cool. 'Look . . . forget it, why don't you, Feathers. For Christ's sake, for us it's holiday time. That's all in the past now. *Finito*.'

'But you were interested in one of the senior partners.'

'Was, Feathers . . . I was interested. You know how the mind runs on. Everything is resolved at this end. If you people want to mess about with figures that's all right by me. Just don't subsidize any more Winters and I'll be happy. I'm happy now.'

'Conclusively, Essington? Was anything shown conclusively in regard to Winter?' It was the lawyer's mind at work. Back-pedalling. Pouring oil on the waters. Juggling with words. Of course that was the way they all got ahead—scratching backs, seeing the other fellow's point of view.

As an automaton for Karen I was struggling to appear a player in the same game. 'Great catalogue, Feathers. The gallery, with that collection, should be . . . well, I can't say a feather in Australia's cap, can I?'

183

'You can and will say what you please, Essington. I know you of old.'

I had selected the table at Pellegrini's for the view. Maybe Nicholls couldn't focus on the distance. He could have caught bad eyes from his economic advisor. Or was he too concerned with the government agencies who were out to swipe his cash? He just did not see his boat.

Half an hour passed crammed full with the smallest small talk. Like exactly when the wind had come up on the previous afternoon.

'Mid-autumn, it starts to blow in from over there.' Mrs Nicholls raised a finger and pointed. Her eyes widened. She squinted a little. Then she turned to her ever-loving Alf.

He was pouring the hundred-and-sixty-franc Chablis down his throat—my hundred and sixty francs.

'That's your tub over there, Alf,' she exclaimed. 'I'd swear it.' She turned to Karen who was watching a dog urinate on the hubcap of a metallic-grey Lamborghini. She touched her on the arm: 'He claims it's his passion, but he doesn't know what the bloody thing looks like.'

Karen smiled enigmatically, as though she hadn't heard a word.

'What's that, Sarah?' You could see that he didn't like women interrupting his thoughtful drinking.

'The boat, Alf. That one out there by the point. It's yours. I'd lay money on it.'

'The boat! Winter's got it, dear. Took it around to San Remo.'

'My foot he did. That's it out there off the point. You wouldn't know it if you fell over it.'

'That yours?' Karen piped up; innocence and enthusiasm. 'That terrific cruiser? Didn't I say to you the other day, Essington, that was the sort of boat I'd like.'

'The other day?' asked Alf Nicholls. 'How long's it been there then?'

'Since I came.'

'And how long's that, dear?' Sarah's face was turning sour.

'Essington?' Karen turned to me for the answer.

'Couple of weeks, maybe more.'

184

'A fortnight?' Nicholls exploded.

'Alf, didn't that girl tell us he was in America?'

'Did she? San Remo, that was what I heard.' His ticker was pumping up the blood. He pulled a bottle out of his jacket pocket, popped a pill. 'So what's it doing here? I'll be damned. He's dumped my boat. The shifty little bugger. He's dumped my bleeding boat.'

'That's what I always said, Alf. Shifty, not a man to be trusted. But you . . . you think the sun shines out of him.'

'Why on earth would he do a thing like that? Dump *Sydney Dreaming*?'

I got another round of visitations from the coppers. Karen was great. She kept on saying how she'd like a lovely cruiser like that. 'You could live on it,' she told them. 'So, why would anyone want to use it as a coffin?'

It was clear that Sophie had taken the death of her boss hard. And it was her final opportunity to stick in the knife. She must have got it into her mind all arse about, with me the baddie who, once arrived on the scene, destroyed the whole set. Maybe the police called her in to make an identification. Someone had filled the head of the investigating officer with every inference and connection possible to embroil the old Essington. I had no trouble picturing her, dressed to the nines, clinging to the raft; the sole survivor. Would she have finally had a clue as to what went wrong? I thought not. For Sophie Vaujour I would remain the ultimate calamity.

The fast-talking Claude Chevet—always available; was I his only client?—took a lead from me and steered the police back towards the Nichollses and the Armitages in their search for explanations. Drugs . . . he popped the idea into their heads. Nothing gets a cop going like drugs. If only in pursuit of a cut.

Chevet kept me innocent.

Wonderful man, Claude Chevet. I feared his account.

Over the months that followed I got to know how the patient feel. I'd read books about men who devoted their lives to capturing just one particular fish. Putting it all into the planning. Then there was General Somebody who retreated across Russia leading Napoleon to his destruction. But you wouldn't have thought of Karen as that type. Not at all. She had appeared to me as somebody content to float along, careless, on the surface of life. And yet, there she was, plotting the moves.

Feathers cooled off. He stopped ringing. Was he content?

In Paris we negotiated with the publisher. He took us to lunch three times. Each time the book became more plush. We were into the vanity-publishing end of the production process; where you pay to get your name on the jacket of a book that might never see the light of the day of distribution. They love books, the French. We were led through detail of the quality of paper, cloths for binding, the subtleties of the tones of gold blocking. We were given options. Karen pressed for spending up. 'Essington, don't you see, it comes off taxable income anyway.' We're all into the game of keeping money from the government. I was learning new ways to think.

It would be sumptuous: silk tweed cloth, hand-marbled endpapers, paper manufactured in an ancient mill near the town of Cahors. The title-page was to be in two colours; then introduction, catalogue and twenty-five reproductions. Aunt's monotypes were to be listed as 'private collection, France'. They were getting a couple of paragraphs all to themselves. The six were to be reproduced.

A thousand copies, bilingual text—French and English. We were aiming at libraries, galleries and collectors. On paper, even at cost, we were liable to do better than break even. That's what the publisher said.

The book was Karen's master move. It was the barb on the hook. Then she began to prepare for the final check. She devised a bait to disguise the barb.

We were walking Desdemona along the beach. It was February. Even the bravest of the brave had abandoned swimming. The sky was overcast. The sand was littered with weed intertwined with flotsam and jetsam. It was a time for strollers to parade silver fox furs.

'Essington, we need to get at the press. To finger these people it has to be ultra public.'

'The media is no problem. That is my only strength.'

'That and your untold wealth.' She threw a stick for the dog who bounded to the sea's edge and there became a timid lady.

'That's if they're still connected.'

'Who's they?' she asked.

'They' . . . Well, Peter couldn't believe his ears.

'I owe you for an omelette.'

'Essington, sweetheart, you owe me for nothing. Anyway, we thought you were in France being ultimately chichi.'

'Where'd you get a cock-and-bull story like that?'

'You know . . . word gets around.'

'Chez Catz? Got a liquor licence yet? Say, with a name like that you ought to pack it up, lock, stock and barrel, and bring it over.'

'Over?'

'Here, France.'

'Christ! Essington, you mean you're ringing all that way to tell me that you owe me for an omelette? Do you know how many eggs a minute international costs?'

'Too well, Peter. All too well. But I've got other things on my mind.'

We talked for over half an hour. He was getting bored with the café anyway; could do with a break. I gave him just enough background to keep him hot. The fee I offered did the rest.

'That's a lot of omelettes!'

'If we pull it off convert it into smoked salmon.'

'Ess, we're not talking bonus money are we? Where's the poor but honest bum we all used to know?'

'It's just honest these days.'

'Half your luck.'

'You certain you can handle it, Peter?'

'They want me in there, Ess. It's touching really, but true. Would you believe they are running short on exposés.'

'So they ought to go for this.'

'Rats up a drainpipe, Ess. They'll love it.'

'And not a word to Gerald Sparrow.'

'Gerald Who? I haven't made him a ham sandwich in months.'

'No, I mean it. That's important.'

'Mum's the word, Ess.'

Peter's job was to ride in on the Ayers Rock Gallery collection. To get inside it. To lure all the donors out into the open to receive their richly deserved public adulation.

Then we'd send him the information for round two.

Even I was getting a feeling for the game.

Karen was in deadly earnest. 'Why?' I asked.

'Don't know. Can't really say. Nothing in particular. Essington, the world is divided into . . .'

'Karen, the world's divided so many ways there's no system for counting them.'

'I don't know then. Only, funny thing . . . in the end it comes down to your old friend Steffano Polini giving me the sack. It was your ex, Annie, pushed him into it. Because of me and you. Because of one night, Essington. I hadn't thought so much of it, like it was nice but it would pass; you'd disappeared. It was a joke, ironical, such a small world. For them it was like I was infected. Maybe I made them feel bad. So I got the boot—bloody casual. For me it was a real blow. I had rent to pay.

'Well, when you told me about your friend Warner and the others, even the hoods, they were only pawns in someone else's game, weren't they? There's no comparison; the scale is completely different. Me and Polini, Italy's gift to plumbing; you and a bunch of killers. Yet the principle's the same, isn't it? They are number one, that's all that counts. They don't care who gets hurt.'

I laughed: 'That's philosophy; Temple and his friends are representative of . . . they are symbols, is that what you mean?'

'Nothing arty farty. Just they deserve what they get.'

Peter managed a full article in the biggest circulation weekend colour supplement. Rosy-cheeked, Temple smiled shyly—the public benefactor. My Degas horses got a small reproduction on account of one of Temple's syndicate being a well-known racing identity. The heading was 'Art's Hidden Patrons'. He must have died laughing writing the piece. A transport magnate was quoted as saying: 'It was a big spirit that built this country. I want to see that spirit born again.'

By early June Peter had them all going. The horse had bolted; most didn't want to miss out on a bit of the glory. They were all up and waving whether they wanted to be or not.

I got a tape of a long radio interview with Jackson and Temple. They told the tale of searching out the nucleus of the collection. Of the long negotiations, the building of the confidence of the unidentified seller who had finally accepted the offer after viewing plans for the new gallery. They quoted the seller as saying: 'Europe is the old world; Australia is the country of the future.'

Temple said: 'You don't knock at a door once. That's not guts. You knock and you keep on knocking.' When asked if he was entertaining the suggestion that he might move from private practice to the public arena, to politics, he said: 'No comment.'

From all the information we were sent, it seems it was quite a syndicate. Quite a catch. Money was pouring in from all quarters to pay for the construction of the gallery. They were to have the most up-to-date lighting system in the world making use of lux-sensitive cells and roof-mounted periscopes.

So the forgeries wouldn't fade.

Peter had spread it all over: 'Australian Art Coup'; 'Buy of the Century'; 'Aussie Moguls Strike Again'. There was a *de facto* auction in progress on the money front. A variety of experts valued and revalued till the figure got into the hundreds. One economics writer stuck his neck out and said that with that kind of connoisseurship and business acumen, Australia could build up security against its national deficit, enriching its culture at the same time. 'From all indications,' he wrote, 'the nation is richer by an estimated two hundred million dollars as a result of this generous gesture.'

Temple must have been kicking himself to have aimed so low. He had written off a mere fifty million on the deal. He could easily have got away with twice that; doubled the size of the consortium.

Deadpan, Rebecca and Renardo watched us rush each morning's mail.

Out of the new Australian cultural euphoria the Paris publisher received forty-seven orders. Degas, it seemed, had become a household word. Otherwise response was poor. I began to add up my loss.

'Essington, it's only money. We're winning, can't you see that? What's a few thousand dollars?'

'A lot of francs.'

'You're impossible.'

We had waited a long time. I had started to lose faith in the ultimate victory.

Then it came.

The books arrived at their Australian destinations between July 1 and July 7. The publisher sent us the list. Miles Jackson, bless him, had ordered three: a man for the big gesture. One went gratis to Peter. The other forty-three were mining the whole field—ready to be consulted.

July 10, Peter got a telephone interview with Grantley Simpson. What he extracted from that was smeared over every newspaper in the country. It was pedantic, detailed information, delivered with perhaps a mock innocence. The case against the Degas was put; it was watertight. It was ten days after the June 30 deadline.

They were caught. The pictures—the whole lot weren't worth the canvas, paint and paper.

A Sunday rag told a more sensational version, the full story, beside a photo of a girl who looked a little cold in nothing but a cowboy hat. (They used to say the bigger the brim the smaller the property.)

For me that piece was a kind of memorial to Clyde Warner. Friend perhaps, mentor certainly.

Under the pseudonym 'Art Fair' Peter had targeted Gerald Sparrow's senior partner. The article kept on harking back to the visit two men had made to Grantley Simpson, testing out a phony Degas.

'Nobody reads those rags, Essington. Only pervs and the lobotomized.'

'Don't you believe it, Karen. That's Peter's *tour de force*, pure journalistic genius. No other paper would have handled it. That article breaks all the rules. People are going to have to follow it up, start asking questions. You had planned to embarrass Temple.

This goes a lot further than that. He'll be lucky not to finish up behind bars; even someone with their brain cut out could identify Temple as the second man in London with the monotype. It's not just a tax scheme gone wrong—not any longer it isn't. There's fraud, and it doesn't take much imagination to work out whose money paid the killers.'

The phone rang. I picked it up. 'Essington?'

'Feathers.'

'Essington . . . have you the least idea of what . . .' He was unable to form words. Never before had Gerald Sparrow been at a loss. I thought I'd help him out.

I hung up.